most promising students. I was hoping you'd help me keep Liam and the others engaged in today's lesson. Do you think you could do that?"

His eyebrows knitted together and he asked, "What can *I* do?"

"For one, you can keep that charming smile of yours ready. I've noticed the girls watching you. Did you know they look away when you say stuff like you did yesterday? But they're quite taken with you when you smile and ask smart questions."

"Oh, uh, okay. I can do that."

***

Dinner at the ranch that night was quieter than usual if you can call only three people talking at the same time instead of eight or nine quieter.

Dawn and Jet chatted with Martha about their visit with the pastor, telling her the relationship exercises he'd assigned them to complete before their next meeting.

Ashley and Corey argued gently over one line of a new song he was writing and Pete and Matt related their difficulties rounding up some of the cattle. Sawyer asked Chris when he thought the little lake would freeze over and Chris, helping himself to seconds of the baked chicken, said it might skim over with thin ice well before Christmas.

"Hey," Blake, farther down the table from Julia tonight, yelled, "teacher-lady, did you get those slackers to toe the line today?"

Julia set down her fork and nodded. "It was Chris's advice that worked. I talked to each kid before he entered the class. No discipline necessary. They were model students today. I only hope it lasts."

Blake's face, which had darkened when she credited Chris, now shifted into a devilish smirk. "I'm not surprised. I had a hot teacher like you when I was in school. I'd've done anything to get into her pants, too."

The hush that fell over the table was instant. Chris rose from his chair, his intention to yank Blake out of his seat and throw him out of the house more than evident by his growl and his own chair falling back.

Martha rose, too. "Chris. Sit down. Blake, please apologize to our guest. I don't know how they talk to women where you come from, but you will be more respectful when you're in my house."

All eyes were on her. It was unheard of for Martha to raise her voice, let alone speak in any tone other than sweet.

Blake's smirk was replaced by a whistle through tight lips. "Whew. Didn't mean nothin' by that, ma'am. Sorry, Ms. Julia." He stuffed a roll in his mouth and started chewing, but there was a glint of defiance in the look he sent Chris.

Chris, seated again, said, "Great dinner, Dawn, as usual." He avoided looking at Julia.

Ashley tried to lighten the mood. "Hey, everyone, I helped Dawn with dessert this afternoon. You're going to love it. Chocolate cake with penuche frosting."

That started the conversations again as several of the guys had never heard of penuche.

Julia kept glancing at Chris until finally their eyes met and she mouthed a silent 'thank you.'

Chapter 12

THE AIR IN the barn was thick with the scent of leather, hay, and the comforting aroma of horses as Chris walked in and headed toward the stable office to speak with Jet and Martha. He could hear their excited voices as they discussed the logistics of the upcoming construction. He reached the half-open door. Jet and Martha were bent over Martha's worn, cluttered desk, examining the blueprint plans and the paperwork for the pole barn. The anticipation of the new addition to the ranch was tangible, but a pressing issue weighed on Chris's mind and he had to interrupt them.

He knocked lightly and pushed open the creaky door the rest of the way, his boots thudding against the wooden floor. His face cued concern and urgency.

"Jet, Martha, we got a wolf problem on our hands. Signs of them are everywhere. And, well, Sawyer called in from the range … they found the remains of a calf the wolves feasted on last night."

Martha looked up, her brow furrowing as alarm etched lines into her face. Jet's eyes narrowed, his rugged features reflecting the gravity of the situation.

"Wolves?" Martha breathed. "On Double Horseshoe land?"

"Yup, it's not normal, I know. But there's been a sudden surge across the state. Missing cattle, pets, chickens. I've seen tracks all around. Probably that's why the herd got split in half the other day."

Jet let out an exasperated breath. "Dang it all. We can't afford to lose more head of cattle, especially not now."

Chris nodded, his hat pulled low against his forehead. He lifted it and ran a hand through his hat-flattened hair, frustrated but determined. "I suppose it might be one of those rare migrations, and they're only passing through. Something's throwing them off their usual patterns."

Martha placed a comforting hand on Chris's arm, her concern evident. "We'll need to be vigilant. Keep a sharp eye out."

"Right, I'll double up patrols. We'll take turns pulling all-nighters."

Jet's eyes focused on the blueprint, deep in thought. He shook his head and then looked Chris in the eye. "Make sure all the cowhands are armed. We don't want to take chances."

"Right." Chris tipped his hat and strode out.

In the stable office, Martha and Jet exchanged glances.

"I think we should tell the girls. I don't want them going out riding alone. Packs tend to stick to their territories. But this ... this feels different." He snorted. "Heck, even walking to the barn might be dangerous."

Martha tucked a strand of gray hair behind one ear. "We can use Duke as an escort."

***

Inside Brew Haven café, the aroma of freshly brewed coffee filled the air as Julia sat at a cozy table with her friends, Emma and Megan. They had gathered for their regular catch-up session, sharing laughs and heart-to-heart conversations, and gossiping about the romance that was keeping Ashley away from them this time.

Julia stirred her coffee, the cup cradled between her hands as she shared tidbits of her life at the Double Horseshoe Ranch. Emma and Megan leaned in, engrossed in her tales.

Julia's face lit up as she related her unique living situation. "It's incredible, really. I've never been around so many cowboys in my life. Each one of them is like a character from a Western movie, and the ranch itself is like something out of a storybook."

Megan chuckled, her eyes dancing with expectation. "Full make-up on for breakfast?"

"Of course. Half the guys come in early, scarf down Dawn's eggs and bacon—some mornings there are cinnamon rolls—and then they gallop off to the range. A couple are there when I eat and whoever's left must come in after I leave for school."

Megan nearly drooled. "A parade of men. How wonderful. What about the evenings?"

Julia's cheeks turned a delicate shade of pink, and she hesitated for a moment before replying. "Well, that's the best time. We all sit down together. Like a family. Six-thirty sharp. At first, most of them looked scruffy. You know, tired and dirty from being on a horse all day, but lately I think they're rushing to shower and show up looking pretty hot."

"For your benefit." Emma nodded her head, grinning. "You are so lucky. Who's the hottest? I mean, I've seen them all either at the rodeo or at the Circle Bar or around town, but not up close."

"There is one in particular."

Emma leaned in closer, her voice tinged with excitement. "Yeah? The one you were drooling over at the rodeo?"

Julia's gaze wandered toward the window, her thoughts drifting to Chris Thornton, the rugged cowboy who had captured her attention weeks ago. Just thinking about him put her heart into a hard cantering rhythm. "Mm-hmm. His name's Chris. He's got this serious charm, and he's always there with a kind word or a helpful gesture. He's given me good advice."

"Describe him."

"Hazel eyes, three-day beard, and a warmth that draws people in. He's ... I guess you'd call him the foreman ... he's in charge of the other cowboys. Chris is ... something else. He's kind, and hardworking, and he really cares about the ranch. He's got a genuine way about him."

Megan and Emma exchanged knowing glances, their smiles widening. It was clear to them that Julia was smitten with this cowboy.

Megan said, "Well, you know, Christmas is just around the corner, and I happen to be hosting an early Christmas party at my townhouse. I've booked the communal room in the clubhouse. Why don't you ask Chris to be your date?"

Julia's eyes widened at the suggestion. She had been wondering how to get their relationship to move on to something other than riding to church with him, but the idea of asking Chris to a party was a leap she wasn't sure she was ready to make. She took a sip of her coffee, her mind racing.

"I'll think about it. I wouldn't want to be too forward ... to impose or make things awkward."

Emma offered a reassuring smile. "Impose? It's the twenty-first century. Women can take the lead."

As they continued to chat, Julia enjoyed the quiver of excitement at the thought of the upcoming Christmas party. Maybe, just maybe, it was time to take a chance on the handsome cowboy who made her heart flutter every time she saw him.

***

Julia was disappointed at supper when three of the cowboys weren't there; Chris was one of them.

Jet explained, "Chris, Blake, and Matt are out with the herd tonight. We've got a problem with wolves."

Ashley, Dawn, and Julia reacted with surprise. Martha nodded briskly. "Don't go outside at night alone. Wolves are generally afraid of humans and the risk of them attacking one of us is low, but … be aware of your surroundings."

The rest of the meal was eaten with less enthusiasm as the conversation stayed serious and each one contemplated the implications.

Later, in Ashley's room, Julia and Ashley talked of happier things. Ashley's relationship with Corey was back on track and Julia relayed Megan and Emma's updates: Megan's boyfriend was still out of town and Emma's was still acting like a jerk. They'd broken up again.

Julia glanced often at the flowers on her dresser. "Are you and Corey going to Megan's party?"

"We sure are. Corey's been warming up on Christmas tunes, in case she asks him to bring his guitar."

"Mm. I was talking with Megan and Emma about the party. I was sort of thinking of asking Chris to go with me."

Ashley clapped her hands together. "About time you made a move. Have you noticed how he looks at you?"

"I have. But he hasn't asked me out yet, well, other than for a sandwich after church. I'm afraid that my apartment will be fixed soon and I won't be seeing him here every day. Out of sight, out of mind. He'll forget about me."

Ashley reached over and plucked one of the flowers from the vase and held the petals to her nose. "Actually ... I was wondering if one or two of the other guys might ask you out this weekend. Would you consider going out with ... uh ... Pete?"

"Pete?" Julia watched Ashley run her fingers down the stem and flick a drop of water off the end. She squinted her eyes at Ashley. "Did he say something to Corey?"

"Sort of. Corey told me that you are a hot topic in the bunkhouse. It was obvious at first that Blake might be in to you, but that's cooled down. I think because one of the other guys has quelled his interest. Maybe told him to back off. It might have been Chris or Pete."

Julia didn't speak for the moments it took for her to wrap her head around the possibility of Pete. The guy, though maybe a little older, was every bit as good-looking, well-mannered, and polite as Chris. He was more the quiet type, but still ... she shook her head. "No, Pete seems nice and all, but I don't think I'd go out with him if he asked."

"Good to know. I'll pass that on to Corey and he can warn Pete so he doesn't embarrass himself."

Julia chuckled. "I'll be the one embarrassing myself if I ask Chris to this party."

"Why don't you get some advice from your secret mentor?"

"Ha!" Julia pulled her phone out of her pocket. "That would be interesting." She scrolled through her texts. "I haven't heard from him today. Did I tell you he admitted to being a cowboy?"

"No way."

"Okay, here goes. I'm going to do it." She read her question aloud to Ashley as she typed: "HEY, THERE'S A

COWBOY I LIKE HERE. ANY ADVICE ON HOW TO ROPE HIM IN?"

Ashley howled with laughter. "Send it."

Julia, her heart aflutter with anticipation, glanced at her phone as a message from her anonymous mentor flashed on the screen only a few moments later.

"WELL, DARLING, YOU'VE GOT THE LASSO OF YOUR CHARM. NOW, JUST BE YOURSELF AND LET THE COWBOY WANDER RIGHT INTO IT. ☺ "

Ashley bounced on the bed. "He sounds awesome. You've got to find out where he lives and who he is."

"Probably some old guy. I'm not going to waste my time when there's a real man right here."

"Okay, then. Well, it looks like your mentor has given you the green light. You can ask Chris. Go get him, cowgirl!"

"Not so fast. I'm going to ask one more thing." Her fingers tapped away and then she read what she wrote: "I WANT TO ASK HIM TO A PARTY. SHOULD I WAIT UNTIL HE ASKS ME OUT FIRST?"

A few moments later the answer came back: "YES."

"Oh ... well ... I wasn't expecting that."

Ashley put the rose back and said, "So ... there's time yet. Maybe he'll ask you out this weekend."

"Or maybe not, with all these night shifts they're riding ... I'm not getting my hopes up. Megan's party is a week and a half away. I guess I'll be going alone."

"You can ride with me and Corey."

Chapter 13

C HRIS SAT ON his bunk, his thumb hovering over his phone screen, a small smirk playing on his lips. He couldn't help but chuckle at his last text to Julia. It was true; he needed to ask her out soon. A sense of exhilaration coursed through him. A chance like this didn't come around every day. But what would she enjoy doing? His hazel eyes glinted as he speculated, the warmth of his room doing little to thaw the chill in his bones from the long day on the range.

As the winter wind howled outside, swirling snowflakes danced by his window. The thought of her had become a gentle blaze in his thoughts, warming him despite the cold Montana night.

Should I ask her out now? Chris pondered, a swirl of nervous excitement building within. He knew he had to seize the moment, yet he was unsure of the kind of date that would resonate with Julia. His mind wandered, envisioning shared laughter and meaningful conversations against a backdrop of starlit skies.

With a sudden resolve, Chris decided to seek advice from his bunkmates. With a deep breath, Chris pushed the door open and strolled into the main area of the bunkhouse, where the other cowboys were gathered. The room was dimly lit, and the air was filled with the earthy scent of leather, sweat, and fresh coffee.

He cleared his throat, breaking the jovial chatter that filled the air.

"Hey, fellas, what do you all do for fun around here? I mean … you know, with … women," Chris asked, attempting a nonchalant tone that concealed the burgeoning butterflies in his stomach.

Sawyer, who was sharpening a knife, glanced up briefly. "Not much, Chris. Just the usual–hitting the bar, catching a movie, or grabbing a bite to eat in town."

Blake, sprawled out on the couch, yawned noisily. "Yeah, not much to do around here."

Pete furrowed his brows, suspicion lacing his tone. "Why're you asking, Chris? You planning on taking someone out?"

Catching the look in Pete's eyes, Chris stumbled over his own words, attempting to steer the conversation away from his newfound interest. "Oh, you know … bored … looking for things to do. Not everything has to revolve around work."

Sawyer looked up, "Well, you could go to the Circle Bar, catch some live music. Corey's singing again. Or there's a new movie in town."

Chase nodded in agreement, adding, "Maybe a nice dinner at that restaurant across from the Brew Haven."

Throughout the suggestions, Pete's gaze remained fixated on Chris. "Yeah, but what if you're thinking about someone special, someone like … Julia? Those ideas won't work for a college grad like her, will they?"

Chris scratched his jaw, trying to play it cool, but his mind raced. "Well, I don't know. Just looking for ideas."

Chris felt the weight of Pete's words settle on his shoulders, the truth undeniable. There was a tension in the room, a silent understanding that maybe they were both interested in the same woman. A gentle conflict swirled beneath the surface, leaving Chris to grapple with his emotions. He would have expected some pushback from Blake, but he'd never considered Pete might be interested in Julia.

Pete's dark eyes bore into Chris, an unspoken challenge between them. "Who's the lucky lady you got in mind?"

"I'd rather not say ... it's someone I've been texting for weeks now." He watched Pete's face look relieved. That wasn't good.

***

The cold night air carried a hushed urgency as Chris hurried back to the ranch house, the quiet crunch of snow under his boots echoing his determined pace. His heart drummed a wild beat in his chest, the prospect of asking Julia out fueling his steps. He knew he had to seize this chance, to unravel the possibilities that seemed to dance in the frosty air.

The night was veiled in a frigid shroud and strange sounds. He scanned the area, remembering the threat of wolves. He thought he saw a dark shape moving near the barn. Probably Duke, he thought as he continued to stride purposefully toward the ranch house. He was excited to see Julia.

As he approached the ranch house, his heart quickened its pace, anticipation mingling with trepidation. He could already envision the warmth of her smile, the sparkle in her eyes, as he posed the question that had been occupying his thoughts when he was on the range. The porch light spilled a soft, inviting glow onto the frozen ground, a beacon drawing him closer.

But as he neared the door, it swung open with a sudden burst of energy, and Martha's voice rang out, summoning her dog. "Duke, come on boy, get inside!" For a moment, the anticipation waned, replaced by confusion as he looked back toward the barn. Duke was nowhere in sight.

"Hey, Martha, I just saw him." He changed course from the side door to bounding up the steps to the front porch, waving in the direction of the stable.

Martha came all the way out, her arms wrapped around herself, and hollered again. "Duke! Come on, Duke!" She looked at Chris. "You don't think he's out running with the wolves, do you? I let him out an hour ago." He shrugged and she added, "I'll bet you're back for seconds on Dawn's apple pie."

Then, he heard it—an anguished whimper, a sound that tugged at his heartstrings. He turned, his eyes searching the surrounding darkness, and there, huddled against the biting cold at the side of the house, was Duke. The dog's normally robust form now appeared forlorn, injured.

"Holy smokes, Martha. I think he's hurt." He rushed back down the steps and went to him. His eyes darted back toward the barn, realizing he'd not seen Duke there a moment ago, but rather a wolf.

Chris knelt beside the wounded canine, his fingers gently probing Duke's body and finding a sticky wet warmth. It was clear that Duke had tangled with that wolf and it hadn't gone well.

"Martha, go inside. I'll take him to the vet," Chris said softly, his voice filled with quiet strength.

As Martha withdrew, her lamentations limited to simple words—"Oh no, oh no"—the porch was repopulated with Ashley and Julia who wanted to see what the commotion was.

"Oh, poor Duke," they both cried as one. Chris lifted Duke gently in his arms, the German Shepherd whimpering.

Julia, her eyes filled with empathy, asked, "Do you need any help?"

The offer was a lifeline. "Yes," Chris replied. "If you wouldn't mind coming along. I'm not exactly sure where the vet clinic is."

"I'll grab my coat."

***

The sterile, fluorescent-lit waiting room of the veterinary clinic enveloped Julia and Chris in a cocoon of tension and worry. The uncomfortable plastic chairs creaked beneath them as they sat side by side, sharing silent moments of apprehension. Their eyes spoke volumes, mirroring the unspoken concern so clearly revealed on their faces.

Julia's fingers clenched and unclenched nervously in her lap. She was anguished for the dog but also desperate to ask Chris a particular question. Her gaze drifted toward him often, finding more to admire about him. His eyes, those enigmatic hazel orbs, stayed focused on the door to the examination room and his fingers kept rotating the edges of the credit card he'd used to pay for whatever was necessary.

"He'll be all right," she whispered to him.

"I hope so. Martha's had him since he was a pup. Got him after her husband died." He pulled out his wallet and inserted the card.

Julia sucked in a whole lungful of air and sighed it out through her nose. "It's hard losing a pet. I had a dog once.

When he died … that was the most crying I've ever done in my life."

"Yeah," Chris put his hand on hers, "same here."

"What if the doctor has to put him down?"

Chris lifted his hand from hers and said, "That's not going to happen. Duke's strong. He can recover. They're only bites."

"Wolf bites." She shook her head and bit her lips. "Duke was the friendliest welcome I got when I came to Double Horseshoe."

Chris huffed a laugh. "Aw, come on, all of us cowboys were friendly, weren't we?"

Their conversation ebbed and flowed like a gentle tide, shifting from their shared worry about Duke's condition to faintly flirty joking.

The veterinarian's sudden appearance brought them both to their feet, and they focused in as if to absorb every word. The news was a mixed bag; relief and concern mingled in the explanation and instructions. Duke had several bites needing stitching and while he would recover, the road to his full health might be a trying one.

"I'd like to keep him overnight," the vet said, "and then you'll have to watch him for signs of rabies. I'll give you a pamphlet on it. Unfortunately, there's no test to diagnose infection. My records show he was vaccinated against it as a pup, but he hasn't been back to receive a re-vaccination since." He raised his eyebrows. "Montana doesn't have a statewide requirement, but it's recommended."

Chris gave a nod. "I'll tell Martha."

Leaving the sterile clinic behind, they stepped out into the crisp winter air. Chris held the door for Julia and she climbed up into the truck's cab easily. Chris started the engine as soon as he got in. It hummed softly, the heater coming on quickly, a soothing contrast to the cold outside. But he didn't put it in gear.

"Martha's heart is going to shatter if Duke has rabies. She'll blame herself."

Julia felt a spurt of adrenaline charge her heart and unexpected words tumbled off her tongue in response, "You know, it couldn't hurt to pray for Duke." She interpreted Chris's look as curious surprise and not ridicule. "I mean … we've been to church together, bowed our heads—at least I did—" she lifted the corners of her mouth, "and we listened to the pastor pray. He said there was nothing too small to ask God for help about."

Chris's smile matched hers in tentativeness and shyness. "Hey, I closed my eyes." His laugh was brief. "Praying is not something I'm good at, but I've heard Martha pray at every supper since I've been here and … yeah … let's pray for Duke." He held a palm out and she set her hand in his. "But you do it."

She got another spike of something—dopamine?—but whether it was from embarrassment or fear or the physical delight of her skin on his, she wasn't sure, but she was glad she hadn't put her gloves on.

"Okay … God, please let Duke be okay and not have rabies … thank you … amen."

Chris squeezed her hand and let it go. "Not bad." He couldn't help but let a small chuckle escape, breaking the solemnity that had gripped them earlier. "So … I guess now we've advanced our, uh, relationship, to a new level." He put the truck in reverse. "Who would've thought a vet visit could count as a second date?" he mused, his eyes twinkling with a playful light. "It does count, doesn't it?"

Julia smiled in response, her heart dancing at the prospect of the connection they were forging. "Well, yeah, I suppose. And not a cheap date, either. Vet bills can cost a fortune."

"Tell me about it."

As they drove away from the clinic, the subject shifted to a brighter note as Chris pointed out the decorations on the stores they passed.

"I love Christmas," Julia said. "Oh, look at those lights." She *oohed* and *ahhed* as they passed a Santa and reindeer display and she found the courage to ask Chris her question. "Uh, my friend ... a friend of Ashley's and mine ... Megan ... is having a Christmas party and I was wondering ... if you'd like to go with me? It's not this Friday, but next."

Without his eyes leaving the road, Chris answered. "Yes, ma'am, I sure would. Now I have a question for you ... another date ... this Saturday ... we can do anything you want. Anything."

Julia pressed back in her seat, more than relieved, and answered, "Absolutely anything? I accept. And I hope that credit card of yours has a high limit." She laughed. "Just kidding."

Chapter 14

JULIA WASN'T AFRAID of getting into a textual tug of war with her nameless phone friend. It was late and she should have been trying to get to sleep. She had school tomorrow and an early before-school department meeting. But she couldn't resist expressing her excitement to her mentor: HEY THERE! YOU WON'T BELIEVE WHAT HAPPENED TODAY. CHRIS ASKED ME OUT! ☺

Julia laughed aloud as she read his response: SO, AT LAST, A NAME FOR THE COWBOY. YOU SURE YOU'RE NOT TOO SOPHISTICATED FOR HIM? ☺

She typed back: YOU SAID YOU'RE A COWBOY. THEY CAN'T BE ALL BAD ☺

TRUE. SO, WHAT'S THE PLAN FOR THE BIG DATE? OR IS THIS THE XMAS PARTY?

Julia smiled. She had two dates to look forward to. She couldn't decide if she'd be more nervous about being alone with him this weekend or being in a crowd with him at a party. She was too slow in responding and a new message popped up: I THINK I'M JEALOUS OF THIS CHRIS GUY. YOU GOTTA GIVE ME SOMETHING. YOUR NAME, AT LEAST.

Julia hesitated, then typed: JULIA. AND YOU HAVE NO REASON TO BE JEALOUS. WE'LL PROBABLY NEVER MEET.

She laid the phone down and undressed for bed. She climbed in and checked her phone one last time. It read: NEVER SAY NEVER. I HAVE COWBOY POWERS. I'M GOING TO TRADE PLACES WITH THIS CHRIS. HE CAN'T POSSIBLY KNOW YOU LIKE I DO.

Julia reread it and tried not to think the texting had gotten a little out of hand. Was she misinterpreting it? This comment seemed on the verge of creepy. She decided not to answer it and set the phone down on the bedside table. She switched out the light and snuggled under the sheets and blankets.

The phone pinged. She looked. SORRY, JULIA, THAT WAS CREEPY. TELL ME WHAT YOUR FAVORITE DATE WOULD BE AND I'LL TELL YOU IF A REAL COWBOY WOULD BE UP FOR IT.

She let the message hang in the digital air for a moment. She had been worrying about that very thing. Chris was country and she was city. She'd been to college and he'd been … well, she'd never asked, but she assumed he'd been riding the range since forever.

OKAY, she typed back, I'D LIKE TO DO AN ESCAPE ROOM CHALLENGE.

She settled back onto the pillow and cradled the phone, her eyes closed. She was almost asleep when several minutes passed and an answer finally came through.

HAD TO LOOK THAT UP. SOUNDS INTERESTING BUT NOT EXACTLY 'RANCH HAND FRIENDLY.' IF HE TAKES YOU THERE, IT MEANS HE'S REALLY INTO YOU.

PROMISE?

I PROMISE. ☺

Chapter 15

THE COLD MONTANA night air seeped into the truck as Julia settled into the passenger seat, her breath forming ephemeral clouds. The dim glow of the ranch house behind them provided a serene backdrop to their third, technically first, date. Chris shut her door and moved around the front of the truck. As he slid into the driver's seat, he dropped his phone into a small cubby hole in the truck's console. He started the engine and cranked up the heat. All she noticed was the musk and spice of his cologne, filling her sense of smell with an expectation of excitement and mystery.

"Well," he said, "everybody here seems to know we're going out."

"Sorry. I told Ashley and Dawn. I'm sure they told Corey and Jet … so they probably spilled the beans to the whole bunkhouse. Martha seemed to already know. Did the guys tease you?"

"Only Blake, and I wouldn't call it teasing. So, where would you like to go tonight?"

Julia hesitated, unsure whether to reveal her penchant for escape rooms, fearing it might seem too unconventional. Her mentor's words flashed before her eyes; the idea that she could gauge how much a guy liked her by his reaction to a quirky date seemed unlikely, but she didn't want to chance making Chris think they were too different to get along. Instead, she chose to play it cool. "I'm not picky," she replied with a faint smile. "As long as it's something we'd both enjoy. You know, like a cow-tipping, axe-throwing, or maybe staking out Big Foot," she teased.

Chris put his hand on the gear shifter and smiled. "Well," he began, and she noted a sly look on his face, "there are some cool things to do in Billings or Bozeman if you're up for a bit of a drive." He paused and his words hung in the air for a moment before he continued. "Like an amusement activity ... I've read they have ... escape rooms."

Julia's heart skipped a beat, her eyes widening in disbelief. It was as if he had plucked her secret desire right from her mind ... or from her texts.

But just as quickly as her thoughts swirled, they stilled as Chris smiled at her with a serious yet tender expression. He took his hand off the gear lever and moved his fingers as if he were about to conjure something out of thin air. "Julia, I need to tell you something."

Her heart did a little dance and she waited, trying not to breathe in the scent of his havoc-making aftershave.

"You're not going to believe this." He picked up his phone and pressed the screen.

She cocked her head ready to hear whatever it was she wasn't going to believe. But her phone pinged. The screen glowed with the same words Chris had just spoken. YOU'RE NOT GOING TO BELIEVE THIS. She looked from the text to his face and back again.

"Wait, what? How did you do that? Oh ... Ashley gave you my number?"

He shook his head. "That's not my first text to you. Scroll up … I'm … you'll see."

She scrolled, saw the many texts between herself and the mentor, couldn't process if he … if Chris … if the mentor was … "I don't understand … How did you …" She looked up as he turned his phone to face her, the same series of recent texts from her nameless friend on *his* screen.

"It's me. I'm him. I'm the guy you've been asking for advice from since September."

Julia couldn't speak. Was this true? Or was it a joke? Another trick. The air in the truck had warmed, but she was downright hot. No, this wasn't a joke. It suddenly made sense. The advice … Corey getting Ashley flowers … the mentor practically guaranteeing he would. Her initial shock gave way to other emotions: surprise and amazement, then embarrassment and a flicker of anger.

"Why? Why didn't you tell me? When did you figure it out? Oh my gosh, you've been playing me!"

"No, no."

A storm of emotions left her irrational; she meant to reach for the door handle, but her muscles wouldn't respond. The atmosphere was abruptly more electric. Hot, very hot. Disbelief and amazement collided in waves. She might be sick. She couldn't look away from his pleading eyes. Then, before she could bring herself out of this numbness, Chris reached over and drew her closer, his lips meeting hers in a kiss that bridged the gap between paralysis and understanding.

Julia, breathless, felt the genuine warmth of his lips, tasted a sweetness that spoke of honesty. He liked her. He'd been nothing but kind and considerate and attentive and … and she liked him. Oh, what a kiss.

The emotions swirling within her shifted again, spinning into a sense of exhilaration and joy; the uncertainty faded.

And the moment stretched. She melted into a second and third kiss, brought her fingers to his cheek and felt his arms encircle her with all that cowboy strength, tempered with restraint.

"I'm not playing you, Julia," Chris pulled back, but kept his arms around her. "I really like you and I think we've gotten to know each other through the texting better than if we just started going out tonight."

Julia still tingled from the kisses, her heart in her throat, her head a mess. "Uh-huh. It all makes sense now. Your advice about my students, about Ashley and Corey, about the Christmas party, you were dropping hints."

"I wanted to tell you right away, as soon as I figured it out, but ..."

All of a sudden Julia didn't care that he'd waited; didn't care about escape rooms or dates; didn't care if the flickering porch light meant several pairs of eyes were watching and wondering why they hadn't pulled away yet. She only cared that she had the perfect guy trying his best to woo her.

"Kiss me again, cowboy, and promise me you'll ..." She didn't get a chance to finish.

"I promise." Chris pulled her in for a longer, sweeter kiss than she'd ever dreamed of.

THE END

Want more?

In book 4, HEARTSTRINGS AND HORSESHOES, we get through the Montana winter with several big events including that Christmas party where something wild happens, and then there's Jet and Dawn's wedding, and … another new romance. Find the next book in the series, HEARTSTRINGS AND HORSESHOES, and find out who captures Pete's heart.

Follow me for new book releases:
https://www.amazon.com/stores/author/B003MX4NCS

Rodeo Romance

by Debra Chapoton
book 2
in the *Hearts Unbridled* series

ISBN: 9798867370404
Imprint: Independently published

Books by Debra Chapoton

Cowboy Romance:
Tangled in Fate's Reins
Rodeo Romance
A Cowboy's Promise
Heartstrings and Horseshoes
Kisses at Sundown
Montana Heaven
Montana Moments
Tamed Heart
Wrangler's Embrace
Moonlight and Spurs
Whispers on the Range

Scottish Romance
The Highlander's Secret Princess
The Highlander's English Maiden
The Highlander's Hidden Castle
The Highlander's Heart of Stone
The Highlander's Forbidden Love

Second Chance Teacher Romance series written under pen name Marlisa Kriscott (Christian themes):

Aaron After School
Sonia's Secret Someone
Melanie's Match
School's Out
Summer School
The Spanish Tutor
A Novel Thing

Christian Non-fiction:
Guided Prayer Journal for Women
Crossing the Scriptures
35 Lessons from the Book of Psalms
Prayer Journal and Bible Study (general)
Prayer Journal and Bible Study in the Gospels
Teens in the Bible
Moms in the Bible
Animals in the Bible
Old Testament Lessons in the Bible
New Testament Lessons in the Bible

Christian Fiction:
Love Contained
Sheltered
The Guardian's Diary
Exodia
Out of Exodia
Spell of the Shadow Dragon
Curse of the Winter Dragon

Young Adult Novels:
A Soul's Kiss
Edge of Escape
Exodia
Out of Exodia
Here Without A Trace
Sheltered
Spell of the Shadow Dragon
Curse of the Winter Dragon
The Girl in the Time Machine
The Guardian's Diary
The Time Bender
The Time Ender
The Time Pacer
The Time Stopper
To Die Upon a Kiss
A Fault of Graves

Children's Books:
The Secret in the Hidden Cave
Mystery's Grave
Bullies and Bears
A Tick in Time
Bigfoot Day, Ninja Night
Nick Bazebahl and Forbidden Tunnels
Nick Bazebahl and the Cartoon Tunnels
Nick Bazebahl and the Fake Witch Tunnels
Nick Bazebahl and the Mining Tunnels
Nick Bazebahl and the Red Tunnels
Nick Bazebahl and the Wormhole Tunnels
Inspirational Bible Verse Coloring Book
ABC Learn to Read Coloring Book
ABC Learn to Read Spanish Coloring Book
Stained Glass Window Coloring Book
Naughty Cat Dotted Grid Notebook
Cute Puppy Graph Paper Notebook
Easy Sudoku for Kids
101 Mandalas Coloring Book
150 Mandalas Coloring Book
Whimsical Cat Mandalas Coloring Book

Non-Fiction:
Brain Power Puzzles (11 volumes)
Building a Log Home in Under a Year
200 Creative Writing Prompts
400 Creative Writing Prompts
Advanced Creative Writing Prompts
Beyond Creative Writing Prompts
300 Plus Teacher Hacks and Tips
How to Blend Families
How to Help Your Child Succeed in School
How to Teach a Foreign Language

Early Readers

The Kindness Parade, The Caring Kids: Spreading Kindness Everywhere

The Colors of Friendship: The Caring Kids, Embracing Diversity

Believe In Yourself, The Caring Kids: Building Self Esteem

Friends With Fur and Feathers: The Caring Kids, Animal Friends

Celebrations All Year Round: The Caring Kids: Our Special Days

Feelings in Full Color: The Caring Kids: A Guide To Feelings

Chapter 1

THE WIND WHISTLED through the small, dusty town of Clearwater, making Corey Johnson wish he'd worn a thicker jacket. Autumn had a firm grip on the region, but today's business couldn't wait. With a determined stride, he pushed open the creaking door of the Clearwater Bank, a place he rarely visited.

As he entered, a gust of air followed him, causing a few customers to shiver and clutch their coats tighter. Corey took a moment to assess the space, his eyes scanning the polished wooden counters, the teller windows, and the dim lighting that seemed to make everything appear colder than it actually was.

His attention was soon captured by the young woman behind one of the teller windows. Her face lit up with a warm smile as she glanced up from her work. Her bright green eyes sparkled with kindness, and a ray of sunlight seemed to find its way to her, even in the gloomy bank.

"Hi there," she greeted him with genuine warmth in her voice. "How can I help you today?"

Corey, in jeans and a denim jacket, suddenly wished he was dressed like one of these businessmen who seemed so sure of themselves. His tight shirt concealed tough and stringy muscles. He was just under six feet tall, lean and lanky.

Corey returned her smile, touched the brim of his sweat-stained Stetson in greeting, and found himself momentarily lost in those welcoming eyes. He cleared his throat, his confident exterior masking his unease. "I'm Corey Johnson," he began, his voice steady. "I've got some questions about my last bank statement. There seems to be an error in my totals."

Ashley, as her nametag revealed, nodded attentively. "Of course, Corey. I'd be happy to assist you. Let's go into one of the private offices." She gestured towards a small, modest glass-enclosed room with two chairs on either side of a computer table.

Corey followed her, settling into a chair and removing his hat as Ashley clicked on the computer. The room was chilly, but her presence seemed to create a pocket of warmth around them. He admired her natural blond hair, her cute face, and her slightly plump figure. That last characteristic was not at all a negative in his eyes.

Their conversation flowed smoothly as Corey explained his financial situation. He'd inherited a small sum from his grandparents and had invested most of it. He expected to see the quarterly dividends deposited, but only his checks from Double Horseshoe Ranch showed up. Ashley listened intently, her green eyes fixed on him, her smile never wavering. She brought his account up on the computer and said, "Look. There they are. Pending. They'll show up on your next statement."

She hit a button and the printer whirred to life, spitting out a sheet with his numbers.

"Well, that was easy." As Corey spoke, he assessed what it was about Ashley that made her stand out. She had a pleasant way about her that put him at ease, and he found himself checking her ring finger.

2

But beneath the surface, he couldn't shake his insecurities. He wondered if she noticed the well-worn bandana tied around his wrist, a token of his cowpoke practicality that contrasted with her polished bank environment. Would she find his rancher's attire off-putting? He hoped his confident facade concealed the uncertainty that churned inside because he wanted to ask her out.

Ashley had more to say: a sales pitch every teller was schooled in giving. She gave a rehearsed spiel about wealth management and offered the bank's credit card. "Or perhaps a debit card would be more to your liking?"

Their conversation continued as she explained a few other of the bank's products and services. To Corey, the coldness of the bank was forgotten as the warmth of their interaction enveloped him. He was drawn in by Ashley's friendly demeanor, secretly hoping that she was prolonging their meeting on purpose.

"Yeah," he said impulsively, "I'll open another credit card. I've got a few things to buy before the rodeo."

"Rodeo? Here in Clearwater?"

"Out at the Double Horseshoe Ranch, about ten miles north." He ran a hand through his straw-colored hair and grinned, counting on his most charming smile to give him an edge. "I've been in charge of setting up most of what's needed. Haven't you seen the flyers around town?"

Ashley blushed. "Mm-hm. I have. Are you competing?"

"Calf roping. It's something I do every day so I ought to be good at it." He set his hat back on his head and reached for a pen. He tore a piece off the statement she'd printed for him and wrote the date and time.

"Come and root for me. I don't have any family in the area to cheer me on so ..."

"Sure, Corey, I'll come. I'll get some friends to come with me. It'll be fun."

Corey nodded. What was wrong with him? Why didn't he just ask her out now? He didn't have any trouble getting a Saturday night date. In fact, he'd just had a second date with a pretty little thing that worked at the Circle Bar, but that wasn't going anywhere.

"Um ... thank you, Miss ..."

"Mumford. Ashley Mumford." She touched her name tag and he was pleased she hadn't corrected the Miss to Mrs.

He and the other cowboys he rode with had been scouring the bars and ranches for marriage-worthy gals when they thought getting hitched was the only way to save the Double Horseshoe. Now that the ranch's legal problems had been solved and the silly marriage condition of the benefactor's money had been resolved, why was he suddenly too afraid or too shy to ask this gal out? He hadn't been this shy around a girl since ninth grade.

He stood up when she did, tipped his hat, and drawled, "Ashley. Nice name. I'll remember it. And don't forget to come." His smile was on automatic; he didn't have to think about it. He only hoped she saw the grin as charming and not arrogant. Arrogance was not a characteristic this Johnson boy ever had.

Chapter 2

A SHLEY STEPPED OUT of the Clearwater Bank, a gentle smile lingering on her lips. The chilled air greeted her, but she hardly noticed it. Her thoughts had been consumed all afternoon by her encounter with Corey Johnson—ten nervous minutes that had sparked a renewed interest in rodeos and cowboys and a certain blonde calf roper. She couldn't wait to meet up with her girlfriends at the cozy coffee shop, Brew Haven, just a few blocks away and tell them about him.

As she pushed open the coffee shop's door, the familiar scent of freshly brewed coffee and the comforting hum of conversation washed over her. A trio of her closest friends, all single like she was, sat at their usual table near the window, chin-wagging and sipping their lattes.

"Hey, Ashley!" Emma called out, waving her over.

Ashley joined her friends, slid into the chair opposite Emma, and allowed herself a school-girl giggle. Her excitement was evident in her eyes. "You won't believe what happened today!"

Megan leaned in with her usual inquisitiveness, her dark eyes sparkling. "What? What? Finally a bank robbery?"

"No." Taking a deep breath, Ashley told of her encounter with Corey Johnson, "Well, I can't tell you why he was in the bank, that's sort of confidential, but ..." deep breath and a sigh, "he is so cute and he told me about the rodeo they're having out at the Double Horseshoe." Her eyes twinkled with enthusiasm. She pulled the piece of paper out and told them the date. All their phones came out and each girl added the rodeo to their calendars.

"Was he cute? I don't think I know Corey Johnson." Emma shrugged her shoulders.

"I haven't seen him in the bank before, but Jet Armstrong works out there, too. Remember him?" Ashley continued, her voice animated. "Anyway, Corey invited me to attend, to cheer for him as he's competing in some of the events."

Her friends exchanged knowing glances, their interest piqued. Emma leaned in closer, her red curls tumbling over her shoulder. "Ashley, you haven't been this excited about a guy in … I can't remember how long."

Ashley's cheeks flushed a delicate shade of pink as she spoke of Corey. She painted a vivid picture of the rancher, describing his light and longish hair, his rugged yet attractive appearance, and the well-worn bandana he had tied around his wrist. To her friends, it was clear that Ashley had already fallen for Corey's charms.

Julia grinned mischievously, her brown eyes dancing with amusement. "Sounds like you've got a crush on this Corey Johnson."

Ashley's smile widened, but a shadow of doubt crossed her features. "That's the thing … it's not like I'm desperate, but … I'm so sick of online dating apps. I felt a connection, a real connection."

"What if he's just a player? What if he's dating someone else?" Megan furrowed her brow in thought. "Um, I saw Denise the other day. She's working at the Circle Bar and she told me she was seeing a cowboy named Corey. I wonder if it's him."

Ashley frowned.

Emma placed a comforting hand on Ashley's arm. "Ashley, don't let that deter you. You're a smart, strong, and talented woman. We'll all go to the rodeo together. If Denise is there, well, you'll know it was just a friendly invitation."

As they chatted about the upcoming rodeo, Megan brought up the possibility of Ashley competing in the ladies' events.

"Oh, I haven't done that in years."

"But you still practice … and it doesn't sound like this is a sanctioned rodeo, just a fund-raiser sort," Emma said, her fingers scrolling through her phone. She found a blurb about Martha Sullivan's Double Horseshoe Ranch hosting a rodeo and read the entry fees aloud. "That's for every event from calf roping to bull riding. And barrel racing is in there, too. A hundred-dollar entry fee. We can all chip in."

"No need. I make fair money at the bank." She gave Megan a pointed look. "Or I could just rob the till."

"Here," Emma said, "use my phone. I'm on their site. You can enter right now. No backing down."

Ashley finished her latte and took Emma's phone, got her credit card out, and filled out the form. She'd been excited just to go to a rodeo, but now, the thought of competing was growing on her. And the thought of being around Corey was positively intoxicating.

Chapter 3

COREY HAD ALWAYS found solace in the bunkhouse at the Double Horseshoe Ranch. The warm camaraderie of the ranch hands, the scent of leather and hay, and the comforting creak of well-worn furniture made it feel like home. He'd been working hard the last few days and had been turning in too tired to pick on his guitar or figure out the melody to the latest song he was writing. As he entered, the chatter of his fellow cowboys surrounded him, but his thoughts were focused on one thing: the upcoming rodeo.

His wiry frame seemed to vibrate with youthful energy as he approached Jet Armstrong, who sat on a worn-out sofa in a t-shirt and boxers, his prosthetic leg a shocking reminder of the man's service to the country. Jet had quickly become the heart and soul of the ranch after Martha hired him last spring. Corey respected him deeply and often sought his advice.

"Hey, Jet," Corey began, trying to appear nonchalant, though his nerves were running wild beneath the surface. "I've got a question about the rodeo."

Jet turned to him. "Shoot, Corey. What's on your mind?"

Corey cleared his throat, his fingers nervously playing with the edge of his bandana. "I'm thinking about entering

8

calf roping, but I'm not sure if I should also give bronc riding a shot. What do you think?"

Jet's eyes flicked down to his prosthetic leg, a silent reminder of his time in the military. "Well," he began, his voice carrying a hint of nostalgia, "I used to do calf roping myself back in the day. But as you know," he added, tapping his prosthetic, "things have changed for me. I'm just getting back in the saddle myself after a long while."

Corey bobbed his head, understanding Jet's unspoken message. He respected Jet's journey and the strength he'd displayed in overcoming his challenges. "So, what's your advice, then?"

Jet leaned back, a faint smile gracing his lips. "Corey, my advice is to do what makes you happy. Compete in the events that make your heart race. That's what rodeos are all about."

Corey had hoped for a definitive answer, but Jet had given him something far more valuable—permission to follow his passion.

As their conversation continued, Corey hesitantly broached another topic that had been weighing on his mind. "There's one more thing, Jet. I've invited a girl from the bank to come watch the rodeo. Would it be all right if I gave her a free ticket?"

Jet raised an eyebrow. "Sure thing, Corey. What's her name?"

Corey hesitated for a moment, then decided to share the name that had been occupying his thoughts all afternoon. "Her name's Ashley."

Jet's expression changed in an instant, a mix of surprise and intrigue flashing across his face. "Ashley Mumford?"

Corey nodded, uncertain about the significance of Jet's reaction. "Yeah, that's her name. Why?"

A slow, knowing smile spread across Jet's lips. "Well, Corey, it looks like you won't need to give her a free ticket. Ashley hit our website a little while ago. She's now entered in the barrel racing event and—"

Corey's heart skipped a beat, and his eyes widened in shock. "She's what?"

Jet chuckled softly, his steel-blue eyes twinkling. "Yup, barrel racing and calf roping. Seems like you've got some competition, cowboy."

As Corey processed the unexpected information, his eyes darted around, and he frowned. "Competition? But she's gotta be in the ladies' events. Barrel racing or …"

"Nope. Not unless we get an onslaught of entries. Girls are going to go head-to-head with the guys in calf roping and some of you guys will have to compete in barrel racing."

"Holy smokes." Corey's face scrunched into a rare expression of confusion. "Looks like I'm going to have to work overtime to teach Tango some new tricks. Do you think an old quarter horse can be trained to race around barrels in just a couple of weeks?"

Jet stretched out on the bunkhouse divan and laughed. "I doubt it, but miracles seem to happen around here."

Chapter 4

A SHLEY'S MOOD WAS light as she walked into the Clearwater Bank, the chill of the crisp morning air still clinging to her. She took a deep breath, readying herself for the day ahead. The bank, with its polished wood counters and rows of teller stations, was beginning to be her daily grind. But today, something felt different.

She headed to her window, her steps echoing through the quiet building. Settling into her chair, she noticed the hushed conversations among her coworkers and the concerned glances exchanged across the room.

Moments later, Mr. Thompson, her boss, approached her. His graying hair and warm brown eyes held an air of empathy, and he wore a sympathetic smile that did little to ease Ashley's apprehension.

"Morning, Ashley," he said gently. "I'd like to have a word with you in my office."

Nerves tingling, Ashley followed Mr. Thompson to his office. They settled into their chairs, and he leaned forward, his expression serious yet compassionate.

"Ashley, I won't beat around the bush," he began. "The bank is going through some changes, and we're looking at reducing our staff. As the employee with the least seniority, I'm afraid your position might be at risk."

Ashley's heart sank. She had never expected this. The bank had been a steady source of income, and the thought of losing her job sent shivers down her spine.

Mr. Thompson continued, "I want you to know that I'm committed to helping you through this. We can discuss your options and see if there's something else that might be a good fit for you."

Ashley nodded, her voice shaky. "Thank you, Mr. Thompson. I appreciate your support." What was she saying? She was thanking the man and he was cutting her throat? A thousand thoughts raced through her head. She couldn't lose this job; this was awful.

Mr. Thompson's gaze softened as he leaned back in his chair, his fingers tented in thought. "Ashley, I've known you for a while now, and I know you have a passion for horses and riding. Have you ever considered turning that passion into a career?"

Ashley blinked in surprise, her thoughts screeching to a halt. A career centered around her love for horses? That was what she'd always wanted, but her counselor in high school and her parents, too, had steered her in other directions. The very idea coming out of her boss's mouth sounded like a dream come true. No, he couldn't have said that. She must be hallucinating. *Get a grip, Ashley.*

Mr. Thompson continued, "There's an old friend of mine, Martha Sullivan, who owns the Double Horseshoe Ranch. She used to teach equestrian events before inheriting the ranch. Perhaps you could talk to her about the possibilities. It might be worth exploring."

Ashley's heart quickened with the idea. Double Horseshoe Ranch. Where the rodeo would be. Where Corey worked. Was she still breathing? There were customers coming in the door, she thought, but she couldn't look that way. She couldn't speak. Mr. Thompson was saying something else, tapping his fingers on the desk. So many things vied for first place in her head ... holy cow ... she never imagined that her love for horses could lead to a career. Gratitude welled up in her as she finally found her voice and thanked Mr. Thompson for the suggestion.

"Of course," he said, "but it's just an idea, a plan B, if you will. I'm working with the Managing Director to save your job, if at all possible." He started scribbling on a piece of paper. "Here's Martha's number and address. I told her you might be out today. Give her a call."

Ashley thought about it all day, called Martha, and felt assured that this might be one of those times when one door closes and another one opens. She left the bank that afternoon, her mind focused on a new path that had suddenly appeared before her. Even if Mr. Thompson could save her position, she might make a change anyway.

When she arrived at Double Horseshoe Ranch, the prairie stretched out before her, vast and welcoming. She parked her car and went up to the ranch house.

The ranch house door swung open, revealing two women. Martha Sullivan, with her warm smile and air of hospitality, wore a comfortable pair of jeans and a rustic denim shirt. Another woman, the cook obviously, was dressed in an apron, her hands covered in flour.

"Hello there!" Martha called out, her voice as welcoming as her smile. "You must be Ashley. I'm Martha, this is Dawn. Please, come on in. I can't wait to talk to you about Bud Thompson's idea." She laughed. "I've always wanted to get back into giving riding lessons. We can be partners."

Ashley felt a wave of relief wash over her as she stepped inside the cozy ranch house. The smell of a home-cooked meal overwhelmed her senses, and she couldn't help but feel that she belonged in this warm and welcoming place. It wasn't much different from the home she'd grown up in. A large, friendly dog came up and she held her hand out for him to sniff.

"That's Duke," Martha said. "You just passed the threat test."

As the three women settled around the kitchen table, they began to discuss the possibilities that lay before Ashley. Martha and Dawn listened attentively as Ashley explained how she'd like to go deep into the world of barrel racing and equestrian events, horse shows and therapy riding, horse boarding and dressage lessons, English riding and Western. Martha was impressed.

"When can you start? It sounds like we'll need a lot of marketing first to get the word out."

"Well," Ashley grinned, "I'm entered in the rodeo. That might be a great place to start advertising."

Martha nodded. "Good idea."

"I know I'm just the cook around here," Dawn said, "and I don't even ride that much." She looked at Ashley. "My fiancé, Jet, has been teaching me, but, anyway, there's one more thing you haven't thought of." She raised her brows and said, "I know you're thinking of the therapy riding for kids with special needs, but you should also consider it for, you know, amputees."

"I hadn't thought of that." In that warm and inviting kitchen, surrounded by the company of new friends, Ashley felt a sense of hope and excitement for the future. The ranch offered her a chance to follow her passion, and she couldn't wait to get started.

"I almost hope Mr. Thompson will fire me tomorrow."

The ladies laughed. Martha asked, "Do you have a horse you're boarding now? A barrel racer? You could keep him here, if you want, no charge."

"I have a mare; she's at my mom and dad's, but thank you, it would be nice to have her here, closer. For some reason my landlord doesn't want her at my apartment." She laughed.

"Oh, save the rent, my dear," Martha said, "and live here. We've plenty of room."

Chapter 5

THE SEPTEMBER SUN bathed the Double Horseshoe Ranch in a golden glow as Ashley stood on the porch, bidding farewell to Dawn and Martha. Martha had invited her to stay for supper with the ranch hands, but she begged off. The thought of eating with seven cowboys was a bit much.

The sprawling landscape stretched before her, a vast expanse of green and blue, and the soft rustling of leaves in the breeze filled the air with a soothing melody.

She gave Martha and then Dawn a quick hug and turned to leave. The thunder of hoofbeats reached her ears, and Ashley's gaze fixed on the horizon. The Double Horseshoe cowboys, riding tall in the saddle, cantered toward the ranch. A single cowboy, broad-shouldered and handsome, came out of the barn to greet them.

"That's my fiancé," Dawn said. "And those are our cowpokes. It'll take them an hour to put their horses away and wash the dirt off themselves. Are you sure you don't want to stay? I made spaghetti. There's always enough. And three cherry pies."

Ashley hesitated, watched the cowboys get closer, and recognized one. Corey Johnson, his golden hair gleaming in the sunlight as he used his hat to whip his horse's flank, led the charge, a confident smile on his face. Ashley felt her heart skip a beat as he reined his horse in, caught sight of her, and trotted over.

"Hey there, Ashley," Corey called out, his eyes twinkling with a vibrant energy. "What are you doing here? Checking out the rodeo grounds? I heard you entered."

Before she could answer Martha put an arm around her shoulder. "Corey, Ashley is my newest hire. She'll be working here in the very near future. So don't go scaring her off with your shenanigans and tricks."

"Who, me?" Corey glanced back at the other men who were dismounting, but keeping curious eyes on the four of them. Corey smiled at Ashley. "Fancy a tour of the ranch?"

A grin spread across Ashley's face as she stepped down from the porch. "I'd love that, Corey." She looked back at Martha. "Mm, maybe I will stay for supper. Thank you."

Corey jumped down and led the horse as the two of them crossed the ranch. Corey introduced Ashley to the other cowboys, each one exuding a unique charm and character. There was Matt, the quiet one with a gentle demeanor, and Chase, the jokester who had a witty remark ready. Pete, with his rugged exterior, seemed to be the softest heart of them all and super shy, while Sawyer's adventurous spirit shone through his every word. She didn't get to meet Jet or Chris as they'd already gone into the bunkhouse.

Corey unsaddled his horse and showed Ashley the stable.

"I might be bringing my horse here … soon." Ashley peered into several of the large stalls. "This place is so clean."

"Yeah, Jet's thorough."

"There are a lot of empty stalls. Martha is thinking of taking in boarders."

"There's plenty of room. Uh," he wiped his forehead with his bandana, "what did she hire you for?"

"Well, it's not final, but … I've always wanted to do more with horses. Teach riders. Teach horses."

"Teach horses?"

"Yeah, you know, barrel racing. It takes a lot of training to get a horse ready for a competition."

"My horse, Tango, might need your coaching."

"Really? I thought you were doing calf roping."

He gave her a happy smirk. "You remembered. Yeah, well, because there are so few ladies entering, we guys are going to have to do some events we're not used to." He patted his horse and closed the gate. "Come on, I'll show you the ring. We're bringing in stands next week. We've sold a ton of tickets already."

"Mm," Ashley nodded. "My friends are coming. Do you know Emma Wright, or Megan McDonnell, or Julia Brown?"

"I don't think so." Corey gestured toward the corral.

"How about a girl named … Denise?"

Corey's head swiveled quickly toward her and he stuttered. "D-Denise? Yeah. A waitress at the Circle Bar."

"I hear she's dating a cowboy. Any idea who?"

Corey's face reddened. "Well, well, uh, I went out with her a couple of times. Odd girl. Not my type." He let his breath out.

Ashley's lips curled up a millimeter.

They walked to the corral and, in sync, put their arms over the top rail and gazed at the barrels that someone, Jet no doubt, had arranged there.

"I think I'll bring my mare over this weekend. It'll be a nice advantage to practice here."

"Mm-hm."

"So, Corey Johnson, tell me something about yourself. Other than your bank account balance ... I know all about that." She stole a glance at him.

"What? You want the story of my life? Okay, my tale begins on a small spread in Illinois. Good family. Church-going type. After high school I set out on a journey to explore the vastness of the great United States." He flung an arm out to express the enormity of his travels. "Years of odd jobs eventually led me to the Double Horseshoe Ranch, where here I am with steady work herding cattle. But," he paused, shook his head, and looked at her, "deep down, my dream is to one day own a cattle ranch of my own. Just like this one."

"Nice dream."

"And you? Other than beating me in barrel racing, which I'm sure you'll do, what are your dreams, Ashley Mumford?"

She played with a sliver of wood on the top rail and said, "I was born and raised on a ranch just outside of Clearwater. I spent my teenage years participating in junior rodeos. I was pretty good." Her laughter echoed through the air as she told Corey about her past accomplishments. "I hope none of that threatens you. I won't bring my trophies; they stay at mom's."

"Hm, well, I think there's definitely going to be a rivalry between us."

"You think?"

"I hope you're ready for some tough competition," Corey teased, his voice playful. "I've got a few tricks up my sleeve."

Ashley's eyes sparkled with mirth as she nudged his shoulder. "We'll see about that. I'm going to need some pointers on calf roping. I know how, but I've never done it in competition."

Laughter charged the air as the two of them continued their friendly banter, their connection growing stronger with each passing moment. The world around them seemed to fade away as they shared more stories, and then Jet appeared and told them it was suppertime.

Chapter 6

SATURDAY MORNING WAS different from other days as half the cowboys took the day off. In the training ring Corey, his brow creased with frustration, stood beside his horse, Tango. He'd been trying for what felt like hours to improve their performance in barrel racing. But Tango, despite his spirited nature, seemed reluctant to cooperate.

Just as Corey contemplated giving up for the day, the sound of an approaching vehicle caught his attention. He turned to see a truck pulling up, a horse trailer in tow. He was surprised to see Ashley in the driver's seat. He tried not to gape as she got out and unloaded a roan mare with a splotch of white on its forehead.

Ashley moved with grace and confidence, her experience with horses evident in every step she took. She saddled the mare efficiently and led her into the ring.

"Hi, Corey."

"Hi."

"This is Star."

"Nice horse. Arabian?"

"Uh-huh. I've had her a long time, but she's still got it when it comes to short sprints. You mind if I get her used to the ring?"

"Not at all. Me and Tango are happy to watch."

21

She mounted and began to trot the horse in easy circles, gradually picking up speed.

Corey watched in awe as Ashley demonstrated her expertise in barrel racing. Star responded to her commands with precision, smoothly weaving through the barrels at a controlled pace. It was a mesmerizing dance between horse and rider, and Corey was captivated by her skill.

More than impressed, Corey couldn't resist a grin. "Wow, that was something else. And you said that was only half-speed?"

Ashley chuckled, her eyes lighting up her face. "Yep, that's right. Star's got a lot more speed in her."

She dismounted and approached Corey with a questioning smile. "How about we trade? You can ride Star a few times to get the feel of it, and I'll take Tango through the course. Teach him a thing or two."

Corey hesitated for a moment. He had never ridden a horse like Star before, and he couldn't deny the fluttering in his chest as he considered the offer, but the fluttering was more from Ashley's presence.

"All right, you've got yourself a deal."

As he mounted Star and took the reins, he could feel the power and agility beneath him. The horse responded to his touch, and they began to circle the barrels, a newfound confidence infusing Corey's every move.

Meanwhile, Ashley took Tango's reins and guided him into position. Once Corey and Star had completed a couple of turns and came back to where she was, she spurred Tango into action. They blazed through the course with incredible speed and precision. The sound of hooves pounding against the ground drummed the air, and Corey was amazed at the transformation of his cow pony.

As Ashley finished her run, Corey dismounted and approached, this time definitely gaping at her. "You're incredible, Ashley. That was amazing."

She flashed him a radiant smile. "Well, thank you, Corey. I've had a lot of practice."

Corey chuckled, feeling an awakening connection between them. As they continued to train, their spirited razzing and witty remarks peppered the air, each comment making the other laugh or, in Corey's case, making him clutch at his throat and feign choking.

An hour and a half later, they were chatting more seriously.

"You know, they say the best views are from the saddle," Corey said, "but I'd argue the best view I've ever had is right here watching you."

"Why, thank you, cowboy."

Just as they were about to wrap up their training session, Jet made his way to the ring, observing their progress. He leaned against the fence and offered a few words of encouragement to Corey.

"Looking good out there, Corey. She's a great teacher," Jet remarked. He nodded at her. "I remember you. Ashley, right?"

She smiled. "Uh huh. And I remember you, too. You've been in the bank several times lately."

Corey looked back and forth between them watching for a connection, but he only saw polite acknowledgement. The swirl of emotion—doubt, jealousy, fear—quashed of its own accord. Ashley's presence had brought out incredibly intense feelings and he briefly wondered if he was getting in over his head and falling too fast.

He watched Ashley race around the barrels once more. Wow, her skill was terribly attractive … attractive and mesmerizing. He absolutely wanted to get to know her better. In the back of his musical mind he was thinking that whether there'd be a love story or a broken heart in his future, he'd have fodder for lyrics.

Chapter 7

ASHLEY OFFICIALLY MOVED into the Double Horseshoe Ranch a week later, her cozy room situated next to Dawn's in the main house. She gave notice to the bank before they could sack her and she left her apartment in better shape than when she got it. The returned security deposit was only enough to hire a truck to take her larger items to her parents' barn for storage, but that was okay. The transition from the bustling bank to the laid-back ranch life was a welcome change, even though her salary was dependent on getting this new endeavor off the ground.

With her personal belongings neatly put away in the second of three guest rooms, she joined the ranch hands and Martha in the final preparations for the upcoming rodeo.

Days turned into evenings filled with laughter and the occasional mishap as they readied the ranch for the big event. Ashley's worries about her uncertain future began to fade amid the warmth of the ranch family and the positive response to their advertisement for riding clients.

One evening, as the sun dipped below the horizon and painted the sky in shades of orange and pink, Corey approached Ashley with a mischievous glint in his eyes. "Ashley, I've got an idea to help you unwind a bit. There's a barn dance happening in the next town, and I was wondering … if you'd like to go with me."

Ashley's eyes brightened at the invitation. "A barn dance sounds like a great way to take a break from all the horse stuff. I'd love to go with you, Corey."

The dance was held in a rustic barn adorned with twinkling string lights, casting a warm and inviting glow. The music swirled around them as they joined the lively crowd, and Ashley marveled at how different this was from her previous life of banking, coffee drinking, and gadding girlfriends.

As they smiled through the line dances and stepped lively to the country and Western music, their chemistry became more apparent. Corey's strong but bashful presence made her feel safe and respected, and she found herself drawn to him in ways she hadn't expected.

Corey leaned in close, his voice a soft murmur against her ear as they danced to a slow tune. "You know, Ashley, I can't help but feel like the luckiest cowboy in the world tonight."

Ashley's heart skipped a beat, and she smiled up at him. "And why's that, cowboy?"

He chuckled, his gaze locked onto hers. "Because I'm dancing with the most beautiful girl in the room, and it feels like time has stopped just for us."

"That's pretty sweet talk for a rough and tough cow hand." She wanted to protest that she wasn't the prettiest and certainly not the slimmest, but she held her tongue.

"Yeah, well, how about this? You must be a lasso because you've got me roped in." He squeezed her a bit closer.

She chuckled lightly and responded, "So … I've got you tied up? Must be because of all that calf roping we've been practicing."

He danced her to a quieter corner of the barn, where they stole a few moments alone. Corey's eyes locked onto hers with a tender intensity, and he brushed a strand of hair from her face. He didn't say a word, but took her hand and led her outside where the band's music seemed to play softly just for them.

"Ashley, there's something I've been wanting to do since I met you in the bank."

Before she could respond, Corey closed the distance between them and pressed his lips to hers in a gentle, lingering kiss. Her heart did a barrel race of its own, and the world seemed to fade away as she let herself melt further into his arms.

Chapter 8

THE DAY HAD been sweltering, unusual for September, the sun beating down mercilessly on Double Horseshoe Ranch. Corey had spent most of it repairing a section of the fence that had been damaged by a fallen tree during the previous night's thunderstorm. As the afternoon sun dipped lower in the sky, a distant rumble of thunder warned of another approaching storm.

Corey glanced up at the darkening horizon, a sense of foreboding settling over him. Clouds like these were associated with thunder and lightning storms and atmospheric instability. He felt both watchful and entranced by the potential fury that nature could throw at them. A storm of this magnitude could spell trouble for the ranch. He hurried back to the ranch house to check on the women there. Jet had beaten him to it. He was busy in the kitchen with Dawn filling gallon jugs with water, expecting a power failure to accompany this second storm.

He found Ashley, Martha, and the dog in the living room watching the weather report on the TV.

Ashley patted the cushion next to her on the couch and, pleased with such an obvious invitation, he sat down next to her, as close as he could.

"Oh brother, I hate the thunder. Do you think it's going to be as bad as last night?" Ashley asked him.

Corey nodded grimly, the memory of the previous night's storm still fresh in his mind. "It's hard to say, but I think we should be ready for anything. We need to round up the horses that are grazing, get them into the barn, and make sure they're safe."

Ashley rose immediately, and they rushed to the stables together, large drops pelting them. Chris and Pete had already begun bringing the horses inside, knowing that the animals would be safer in the shelter of the barn. The tension in the air was evident as more raindrops began to fall.

Inside the barn, the horses were restless. Corey and Ashley worked quickly, calming the skittish animals, and securing them in their stalls. The sound of rain drumming on the roof grew louder, and flashes of lightning seen through the open barn door illuminated the darkened sky. Chris and Pete grabbed a couple of rain ponchos, intending to head back to the ranch house as soon as the last stall was closed.

"You two coming?" Pete yelled over the noise of the storm.

Ashley's horse, Star, was whinnying and kicking at the stall boards. "I'm staying with Star."

"I'm staying with Ashley," Corey said. "You guys go on. I'll close the barn door behind you."

As Ashley worked to calm Star, Corey stole glances at her. Her hair was slightly disheveled, strands clinging to her face with sweat and rain. Her determined expression was an indication of her dedication to her brand-new job at the ranch and to her horse. Corey admired that.

The storm raged on outside, the wind howling and rain attacking the barn walls. Ashley and Corey looked at each other and she motioned for him to come into the stall with her. Together they huddled next to Star, discussing their options, and wondering about the livestock out on the prairie. The interior lights flickered and though that didn't seem to upset any of the horses as much as the thunder and lightning, it made Ashley gasp.

She stroked Star's neck and said to Corey, "What if the power goes out?"

"There's a generator. Don't worry. We've had to use it before."

"I had to stay in my folks' barn all night once when Star was sick. I can bed down here if you want to go back to the ranch house and get some dinner."

"Hey, little lady, I'm not about to let you stay here alone … or starve to death. I'll bet you've never been in the second tack room, Martha's office, where there's a fridge and a cupboard full of snacks. You want something?"

She shook her head.

"Then neither do I."

The sky opened up further and it sounded as if a million gallons fell all at once. Ashley gave Corey a fake smile and moved into his arms.

"Ah, now this is where you ought to spend more time." He kissed the top of her head and cuddled her tightly. "You aren't by any chance afraid of storms, are you?"

"Maybe a little." She tilted her head up and looked into his eyes. "Just hold me."

"With pleasure." He focused on her eyes, the way her hair looked, slicked back and wet, and the slight freckling on the bridge of her nose.

He enjoyed the feel of her, all softness and flower-scented. He liked how holding her made him feel. He'd had girlfriends before, but none had brought out in him this new reaction that he needed to be the protector, the knight, the rescuer, the one to make bad things bearable.

She tucked her head down against his shoulder, her face under his chin, and whispered, "I like this."

"Mm-hm. Me too."

She giggled. "It's a shame I'm going to have to embarrass you in both the barrel racing *and* the calf roping."

Corey chuckled. "Don't worry about it." He put a finger under her chin and tilted her face back up. "But if you think it might change things between us—one of us beating the other in *her* event—then we better take advantage of this storm …" he tipped his face down "and enjoy ourselves while we're both still the best at something."

"And that something is …?"

He kissed her gently, soundly, then with a bit more passion, their lips warm and wet, tongues seeking, hearts pounding.

Chapter 9

FINALLY, THE DAY they had all been waiting for arrived: the Double Horseshoe rodeo. The ranch bustled with excitement as people from the nearby town and surrounding areas flooded in to witness the competitions. The atmosphere was electric, charged with the energy of eager spectators and the scent of delicious things wafting through the air. Matt, with Martha's help, had hired several food trucks and Dawn had set up her own stand of baked goods.

Chase, in charge of tickets and promotions, had lined the fences with banners advertising their sponsors. The stands were already full with dozens more spectators finding spots along the fence to watch or they were munching on corn dogs or devouring burgers laden with huckleberry barbecue sauce. The afternoon sky was clear, the sun casting its own spotlight on the rodeo arena.

Ashley handed out flyers publicizing the new riding program at Double Horseshoe.

Jet, seated in the announcer's booth, raised his microphone to his lips, his voice filled with enthusiasm. "Ladies and gentlemen, welcome to the Double Horseshoe Ranch Rodeo! We've got a fantastic lineup of events for you today, and it's going to be wild!"

There were two dozen contestants including six of the ranch's cowboys. They all observed rodeo superstitions: none wore yellow, no one had bought a new hat, and each had emptied his pockets of change, leaving it all in a jar in the bunkhouse for good luck. The Double Horseshoe boys shook each other's hands, patted backs, gave encouragement, and then either readied their horses or gathered with the other contestants to watch.

Ashley's friends, Emma, Megan, and Julia, were in the stands too, waving handkerchiefs imprinted with double horseshoes and shouting their lungs out.

In the heart of the action, Corey and Ashley stood side by side, their nervousness and excitement palpable. Jet's voice boomed through the speakers, introducing the first event—bronc riding. Ten riders, including Pete and Chris, prepared to showcase their skill and bravery.

The gate swung open, and the broncs burst into action, sending riders flying through the air in a thrilling display of grit and strength.

On the first jump out of the chute, Pete had the heels of his boots above the horse's shoulders before its front legs hit the ground. The crowd cheered and the judges gave him a score that the following contestants would have a hard time beating.

The broncs were fierce, bucking and twisting in a desperate attempt to unseat their riders. Dust swirled in the air as the riders clung on for dear life. The crowd roared loudest for Chris, but in the end, it was Pete who won.

Next came calf roping, a test of precision and speed. Ashley, along with two other determined girls, and six guys including Chase and Corey, took their positions. The calves were let loose, dashing across the arena in a blur. Ropes whistled through the air as the competitors displayed their mastery, skillfully catching and restraining the calves.

Corey's heart raced with anticipation as he waited for the calf to dart from the chute. With lightning-fast reflexes, he swung his lasso, the rope snaking through the air and capturing the calf's hind legs. The crowd roared with approval as he skillfully tied off his catch.

Corey did well, but Ashley, next up, did not. She fumbled the rope. She laughed it off, waved at the crowd, and received a smattering of applause and cheers, mostly from her girlfriends.

"Tough luck, Ash." Corey held her horse as she dismounted.

"It's okay. I didn't expect to match your skills. You do it every day." She took the ends of the reins from him and smiled. "Just wait. I'll even things out in the barrel racing."

Corey nodded. "I know you will. For all my practice I've only gotten under twenty-three seconds once."

Ashley laughed and shook her head. "That should be easy for me and Star to beat."

In the middle of the bustling competition, they found this moment to stare at each other, touch hands, and smile. Maybe they heard Jet's announcement, maybe not, but it was Corey he named as winning the calf-roping, with Sawyer a close second.

The banners began to flap in a sudden fall breeze. The scent of hay and dust swirled in the air, mingling with the tantalizing aroma of sizzling barbecue.

At last, the barrel racing event began. Three out-of-town girls competed before it was Corey's turn. Ashley held her breath as he thundered down the arena, his horse maneuvering through the tight pattern of barrels.

Jet announced his time: "That was twenty point four seconds, folks. Good job, Corey Johnson. That puts him in fourth place," Jet chuckled into the microphone, "out of four contestants with one more to go. Let's hear it for our final barrel racer, Miss Ashley Mumford of the Double Horseshoe Ranch."

The thunderous applause and shouts of encouragement filled the air, adding to the adrenaline-fueled atmosphere. Ashley reined Star into position and let herself scan the stands for her parents. There they were, sitting right behind her former boss, the banker Mr. Thompson. She quickly dismissed him, her parents, her girlfriends, and all the spectators, including Corey, as she focused her concentration on what she and her horse were about to do.

Corey stayed mounted just outside the fence where he could watch. He shouted the loudest when she took off. He could see right away the connection she had with her horse. Star took off fast and slowed just the right amount to circle the first barrel and keep on balance. They raced to the second barrel, another right-handed circling, and then on to the third for a left-handed turn and on to the finish line.

Corey rose in his stirrups and shouted, lifting a fist and waving that bandana he always had tied there.

Jet's voice boomed. "Whoa, folks, that was an amazing seventeen point two seconds. We have a winner. Congratulations, Ashley Mumford."

Panting, Ashley waved to the crowd and trotted out toward Corey.

"You've been holding back," Corey said, leaning out as their horses walked toward the barn side by side. "That was unbelievable."

They dismounted at the barn and led their horses inside.

Meanwhile, the bull riding event had the crowd on the edge of their seats. Matt, Chase, Sawyer, and Pete flaunted their courage as they mounted the mighty bulls. The tension was unmistakable as the gates swung open, releasing the powerful beasts into the arena. Each ride was a fierce battle of wills.

Jet kept the crowd engaged with his spirited commentary, heightening the excitement of the final event.

In the stands, Dawn and Martha nervously watched, their hearts swelling with pride at the courage and skills of their ranch family.

But inside the barn, the sounds and smells of the rodeo were muted, ignored, and forgotten as Corey took a seat on a bale of hay and pulled Ashley onto his lap.

"Hey," Ashley put her arms around his neck, "we're going to miss the ceremony where they give out the belt buckles."

"Mm-hm."

"And my parents are here … you want to meet them?"

"Later."

Chapter 10

THE RODEO ENDED in a spectacular display of fireworks that painted the night sky with bursts of vivid colors. Corey and Ashley joined the other competitors at the fence and stood side by side, their faces illuminated by the dazzling lights as they watched the shimmering spectacle.

Most people were *oohing* and *ahhing*, but Corey and Ashley fell silent, exchanging smiles then looking skyward. Their fingers brushed against each other as they soaked in the magic of the night.

Pete and Chris, always quick to tease, couldn't resist a playful jab. "Aw, did we miss something special during the closing ceremony?" Pete grinned mischievously.

Chris chimed in with a sly wink, "Yeah, I think Corey and Ashley found their own fireworks in the barn. We're lucky they didn't burn it down."

Corey felt his cheeks flush with embarrassment, but Ashley simply laughed, her eyes twinkling with delight. "You guys have quite the imagination," she teased back.

Just then, Jet and Dawn approached, their presence commanding respect from the rowdy cowboys. Jet, with a subtle smile, handed Corey and Ashley their well-earned winnings. "You both did a fantastic job tonight. Ignore these troublemakers," he said, gesturing to Pete and Chris. "You've earned every bit of this."

Dawn stepped closer. "We're so proud of both of you."

The teasing subsided and the night continued with laughter, music, and recounting of bull rides and bronc busting, but Corey and Ashley remained in their own world, their connection deepening.

As the final firework painted the sky in a brilliant cascade of colors, the crowd began to disperse, heading back to town or home. Ashley's friends gave their farewells with words of congratulations and sidelong glances and approving looks at Corey. Her parents slipped away with nothing more than a wave and two grins.

Martha asked all the ranch hands to come up to the house for a tally of the money raised. Corey and Ashley lingered at the corral and leaned against the rails, watching the others go on.

"I don't want the day to end," Ashley sighed.

"Me neither … but … we'd better get up there. You know we had this rodeo to raise money to save the ranch, but now we don't need it. Martha said she'd split it with all of us."

"Really?"

"Yeah. I'm sure you're included. Come on."

Corey walked Ashley to the ranch house, the crunch of gravel beneath their boots the only sound in the now quiet night.

On the porch, under the soft glow of the porch light, Corey turned to Ashley. "I had an amazing time today," he said, his voice gentle.

Ashley's heart skipped a beat. "Me too, Corey. I was so proud of you."

He hesitated for a moment, then gathered his courage. "Would you like to go on another date? Maybe a trail ride tomorrow, after we help clean up from the rodeo?"

A smile spread across Ashley's face. "I'd love that, Corey."

The door burst open and Martha stood there beaming. "Hey, you two, get in here. There's more than money being handed out."

Corey's brows knitted together.

Martha grinned. "Yeah, Jet and Dawn are handing out invitations. They're getting hitched the first day of January!"

Chapter 11

ASHLEY AND COREY enjoyed themselves on a picturesque trail ride on Sunday morning, she on Star and he on Tango. The dog, Duke, followed them for a short way and then turned back. They were headed to a small, secluded lake hidden away in the heart of the ranch, a perfect spot for a romantic picnic.

"I feel a little guilty not going to church with Martha and Dawn. Jet comes with us, too, now." Ashley kept one hand on the picnic basket tied to her pommel and the other hand twitched Star's reins.

"Martha asks us guys every week. I'll get there eventually."

"It's a nice church. Wonderful worship service. Lots of nice sinners," she laughed. "I love the praise songs we sing."

"Yeah, well, we can worship the Lord out in Montana's magnificent nature." Corey kept his horse from getting ahead of Star. "You like to sing?"

"I do."

Corey had brought his guitar along, strapped right behind his saddle, wiggling on Tango's rump. They rode side by side, the horses' hooves creating a rhythmic cadence.

At the lake's edge, they dismounted, Ashley spread out the blanket and Corey gently placed his guitar on it. He squatted down, unzipped the case, and let his fingers hover over the strings. "I've had a tune in my head," he confessed, his voice filled with self-doubt, "but I can't seem to find the right lyrics."

"Let me hear it," Ashley said, her encouragement warm and inviting. She put the picnic basket on the corner of the blanket and sat down cross-legged. She'd had her hair up in a clip, but she let it down and shook out the blonde waves.

Now even more nervous, Corey picked up the guitar, sat down on the blanket, and began to sing:

"In the heart of the West, where the tumbleweeds twirl,
A lonesome cowboy dreamt of a banker girl.
Underneath the stars, in the moon's soft embrace,
They found love's rhythm in this vast, open space."

Ashley's heart swelled with sudden emotion as the words hung in the air, but she had to laugh. "That was … was …"

"Terrible?"

"Uh, yeah."

She hummed his tune. "It's catchy. I like it. Maybe if we—"

"We?"

"Yeah, you could use a co-writer."

He plucked out the tune again. "Okay, what're your lyrics?"

"Change the West to Montana and the first line is okay."

He sang the four lines again slowing it down to try out her suggestion.

"Yeah, much better … except for the last line. Let's work on that."

Inspired, they began to toss rhymes back and forth, their laughter ringing through the serene landscape. Her voice joined his in harmony with the new lyrics. They tried to outdo each other with crazy and humorous rhymes, their creativity flowing like the gentle breeze that rustled the leaves around them.

"That was great, but … I'm going to give it a little more work." Corey strummed a final chord and then set the guitar back into its case. Ashley opened the picnic basket and set their food out. They ate and laughed and talked. They shared their impressions of yesterday's rodeo and then returned to making up song lyrics.

But as the day waned, the late September air turned chilly, and the sun went under the clouds. "I think we've exhausted our rhyming abilities," Corey admitted, his eyes glimmering with mirth, one hand pushing the guitar case completely off the blanket.

Ashley nodded in agreement, feeling a shiver run up her arms. "Maybe we should save the rest of the song for another day."

With a fresh gleam in his eye, Corey stretched to push the basket off the blanket, too. He ended up lying across the blanket, head on one end, boots off the other.

"Get in my arms. I'll warm you up." He held his arms out and she smiled as she laid herself next to him. They both laughed as he rolled them into a burrito, the blanket covering them from head to toe, their giggles and kisses muffled in the warmth.

Their intimate snuggling had a melody of baritone hums and alto purrs. Occasional lyrics included words of flattery.

"You have the prettiest eyes," Corey murmured and kissed each lid.

"And I like your nose." Ashley ran a finger down the bridge of his nose, her head now tilted back and her eyes open. But they quickly closed as he pulled her in for another kiss. The pleasant caresses and sweet words went on for quite a while with no pressure to advance; they simply enjoyed the smooching.

Eventually, they unwrapped themselves from their warm cocoon and stood up. As Corey reached for his guitar, his phone slipped from his pocket and tumbled to the ground.

Ashley picked it up for him just as it beeped. She automatically scanned the screen and read the beginning of a text from a sender named Denise, and her heart sank.

Chapter 12

THE COZY AROMA of freshly brewed coffee permeated the air as Ashley sat with her friends, Julia, Megan, and Emma, at their favorite corner table in the Brew Haven café. It had been two days since the rodeo, and they were eager to catch up.

"You were awesome!" Megan said. "I've never seen anyone ride like that before. I loved the rodeo."

"Yeah," Julia agreed, "you were great. Too bad about that calf roping event, though. It must have been nerve-wracking to compete against guys like that."

Ashley smiled, shrugged her shoulders a bit, and said, "Thanks. And yeah, I was pretty nervous about the roping. But they needed more entries for the events and so …"

"Oh," Emma said, "I wondered why there were always some, shall we say, low achievers in each event. It was a good thing my boyfriend couldn't make it. He would've been unjustly heckling and yelling at them."

Julia rolled her eyes; none of the girls approved of Emma's boyfriend, Jason who, when Emma wasn't around, they called 'the jerk.' Julia finished her eye roll and said, "So, come on, Ashley. Tell us about these cowboys at the ranch. I especially want to know about that one with the dark curly hair that bounced wildly every time he lifted his hat to wave it."

Ashley laughed, glancing down at her coffee cup. "Well, they're quite a bunch. Chris, the one you're thinking of, Chris Thornton, is the tall, silent type. He's got clear hazel eyes and an easy warmth that draws you in. He always wears that old cowboy hat at a jaunty angle."

"Sounds yummy," Julia sighed.

"Then there's Pete. He's a bit of a charmer, and Chase is always cracking jokes. And the announcer, Jet—you wouldn't know it because he hides it so well, but he's an amputee. Our cook, Dawn, just got engaged to him. They're really nice."

Megan leaned forward, her eyes bright with curiosity. "And Corey?"

A wistful smile graced Ashley's lips. "Corey is amazing. He's so genuine and caring, not to mention incredibly talented." She paused and grinned. "And a great kisser."

Megan gave her a friendly shove. "Better at kissing than he was at that barrel racing?"

"Hey, come on. He really put an effort in on that. It wasn't his thing. He did better at that than I did trying his specialty—calf roping."

Emma nudged Ashley good-naturedly. "Sounds like you've really got a thing for him."

Megan added, "Yeah, we want more details. Sounds like a lot of sparks are flying."

Ashley blushed, her gaze drifting to the window. "Yeah, they were. We went on a picnic Sunday."

Julia leaned in closer. "And? That's where all this kissing took place?"

Ashley chuckled, her cheeks turning a faint shade of pink. "Mm-hm. And he sang a song for me. He plays the guitar and …" Ashley hesitated, her thoughts drifting to the text she had seen on Corey's phone. She finally decided to share her worries. "I'm just afraid there might be someone else. I saw a text on his phone from that girl, Denise, and it's been bothering me."

Megan's brow dipped into a pucker of concern. "I knew it. I told you Denise was seeing a guy named Corey. What did the text say?"

Ashley had no trouble recalling the exact words, her memory sharp under the weight of her worry. "It said 'THURSDAY NITE, 7:30.'"

Emma sighed. "Maybe it's just a reservation or something. We should give Corey the benefit of the doubt. Did he ask you out for Thursday?"

Ashley shook her head.

Megan set her jaw and scowled. Julia put a reassuring hand on Ashley's arm and told her not to worry about it.

But doubts clouded Ashley's mind. She was falling for Corey, and the thought of competition made her uneasy. "I just want to know where I stand," she confessed, her vulnerability showing.

Julia nodded in understanding. "Then let's find out. We'll go to the Circle Bar on Thursday night and see what's really going on."

Agreeing with the plan, the group continued with their conversation, though Julia kept looking at her phone to read and then respond to several texts.

"Is that your phantom boyfriend?" Ashley teased.

"Just some shy guy I've never met and probably never will. I only know him as a phone number. But if things don't work out for you with Corey, I'll see if he has a friend."

Ashley laughed. "Nah, no thanks, it's probably some scammer on the other side of the world."

The conversation meandered then from catfishing to online dating to rodeo stories to Julia's classes to Ashley's growing number of clients for her riding school. But Ashley's mind remained preoccupied with the looming uncertainties about her budding romance with Corey.

Chapter 13

MISSED YOU AT supper last night," Sawyer said to Ashley as the cowboys filed into Martha's large dining room and took their seats.

"I was out with some girlfriends," she answered, avoiding looking at Corey.

Corey sat at one end of the table, casting sidelong glances toward Ashley, who was at the opposite end, between Sawyer and Martha. He had tried several times to catch her attention during the meal, but she steadfastly avoided his gaze, her focus solely on her plate, or when necessary, on Martha or Sawyer.

The cowboys regaled each other with tales of the day's work, peppered with mocking and teasing. They discussed the mishap when one of the men had taken an unexpected tumble from his horse during the cattle roundup. The men were relieved the spill hadn't been worse. This was the wrong time to lose a member of the team. Everyone was needed to herd the hundred head of cattle to new grazing pastures.

Sawyer whispered something to Ashley and she laughed. Corey, from the other end of the table, frowned. It happened twice more and he was ticked.

Dessert was served, a delightful chocolate layer cake prepared by Dawn. It should have been a sweet ending to the meal, but several of the men noticed the awkward tension between Corey and Ashley.

After the last crumbs had been devoured, the cowboys began to amble back to the bunkhouse, except for Jet who always helped Dawn in the kitchen, and Corey, who followed Ashley and Martha to the living room. Martha picked up a quilting project and Ashley sat next to her to help sew.

Corey hesitated, then entered the room. He sat down and struggled to strike up a conversation with the two women, but the words came out stilted and awkward. The atmosphere felt tense and knotty, even the dog was ignoring him.

"Ash," he finally said when short phrases about the weather or horse feed got him nowhere.

Ashley looked up briefly, offering a polite smile, but her attention quickly returned to her stitching. "What, Corey?"

Corey fidgeted, laboring to find the right words. "How was your day?"

"It was good. Three new riding students for me and two for Martha." Ashley replied, her voice polite but distant.

Corey sighed internally, feeling the increasing rift between them.

Ashley kept her gaze fixed on her work, responding primarily to Martha's comments, and ignoring Corey's attempts at communication. It was as if an invisible wall had risen between them.

Frustration welled up inside him, and he abruptly stood, muttering something unintelligible. Without a second glance, Corey turned on his heel and skulked out of the room, heading back to the bunkhouse. Completely confused.

Martha watched him go, a puzzled expression on her face. Once Corey was out of earshot, she turned to Ashley, concerned. "What's going on between you two?"

Ashley sighed, her fingers stilling on the quilt. "I like him, Martha, but I can't shake the feeling that he's playing the field, seeing other women. I don't want to be just another name on his list."

Martha squinted thoughtfully. "Well, why don't you talk to him about it? Communication is key in any relationship."

Ashley nodded, her gaze distant. "You're right, Martha. I should. I just ... I don't want to get hurt."

Martha placed a motherly hand on her shoulder. "Sometimes, taking that risk is worth it, dear. But you'll never know unless you talk to him."

Chapter 14

FRUSTRATED AND RATTLED, Corey stormed into the bunkhouse. A couple of the guys were in the lounge, boots off, but hats still firmly on their heads, watching a sports game on TV.

Sawyer looked up and teased Corey, "Hey, dude, did you strike out with the barrel racing champ? Or what?" He nudged his buddy and laughed.

Corey stomped toward him. "What'd you think you were doing, Sawyer? I saw you. At supper. Getting a little too friendly with Ashley. You know, I'm ..."

"What?" Sawyer jumped up, his stocking feet slipping a little as he waved a fist in Corey's face. "If you're dating her, say it. If you're getting all hot and heavy, that's one thing, but if she's just teaching you barrel racing, that's another. She's fair game."

Corey lunged at Sawyer and they both went down on the couch, swinging and swearing.

Chris threw down the remote, grabbed Corey by the shoulders, and pulled him off Sawyer.

"Settle down. Hey! We're a team. Act like it."

"He needs to back off," Corey growled, trying to keep his temper in check. He was on edge, every nerve screaming, ready to defend his feelings for Ashley.

Sawyer wasn't one to back down easily, and the tension in the room escalated as they exchanged heated words. Their voices clashed like thunder in a storm, filling the bunkhouse with a charged energy. It was a clash of wills neither wanted to surrender. And Chris was still in the middle, holding both of them back.

"I said that's enough. Corey, go on to your room. Cool down."

Corey shook Chris's hand off him and, still simmering with anger, retreated to his room. He needed to calm down, to escape the storm brewing inside him. Why was Ashley suddenly so distant? He'd noticed something amiss on the ride back from the picnic Sunday. She kept Star in front of him and his horse and never slowed down. She only said two words when they got to the barn. He didn't understand. They'd been having such a good time.

He slammed the bedroom door shut, the anger burning in his chest. His room was small and cozy, the walls adorned with weathered posters of his favorite country musicians. The soft glow of a desk lamp cast a warm, amber hue over the space. He glanced at his guitar propped against the wall, the polished wood catching the light.

He paced his tiny room then took the guitar, an old friend, its wooden body worn and battered, and started strumming. The smooth notes filled the room with a relaxing rhythm. It was a good way for him to channel his emotions, to find peace amid the anger. The gentle strokes of the guitar strings seemed to calm the tumultuous tempest within him. And … he really needed to practice. He had a gig tomorrow.

He strummed softly, the sound resonating with an almost therapeutic quality. The melody was simple, soothing.

As he played, the emotions of the day flowed into the music. He changed the words that had been swirling in his mind since his picnic with Ashley.

"You're breakin' my heart, why can't you see?
You're the one who sets my soul free.
I can't help the way I feel inside,
But I'm scared to let love be my guide."

The chords reverberated through the room, the heartfelt lyrics echoing his inner turmoil. With each note, he poured his emotions into the song, the melody a soothing balm for his wounded pride and the uncertainty that had clouded his feelings for Ashley.

"Sometimes love's a risk we take,
But darling, for your sake,
I'll lay it all on the line,
If you'd only be mine.
You're breakin' my heart, can't you see?
Lost in your world, longing to be free.
Every glance, every smile, just a sign.
Why can't you be mine?"

Corey sang softly. Each chord resonated with the feelings he struggled to express. The melody was a comfort for his soul, a salve for his confused heart.

As he played, the turmoil that had gripped him began to subside. The adrenaline from his earlier encounter with Sawyer diminished. The music washed over him, carrying away the weight of the feud, the anxiety, the lack of confidence. In this sanctuary of sound, he found solace, and a spark of hope reignited within him.

Perhaps, if he finished the song for her, he could bridge the gap, and find a way to reconnect. He continued strumming, the melody echoing through the bunkhouse.

Corey knew he had to talk to Ashley, to clear the air, to get an answer as to why she was suddenly aloof, and to lay his feelings bare.

With a sigh, he continued to play, his fingers dancing across the strings, composing a love song that he hoped would find its way to Ashley's heart.

Chapter 15

THE CIRCLE BAR buzzed with the chatter and laughter of its patrons. Ashley and her friends had settled into a corner table, their hushed conversations punctuated by occasional bursts of raucous laughter from nearby groups. Megan couldn't resist pointing out her friend, Denise, a waitress who was working diligently among the patrons.

"She's the one," Megan whispered with a mischievous grin, gesturing toward Denise. "That must be who sent Corey that text."

Ashley hesitated, watching Denise as she flitted between tables. She looked familiar, but Ashley couldn't place her. Something about her demeanor struck Ashley as genuine, and she didn't want to jump to conclusions.

"I think I've seen her at church," Ashley replied cautiously, unwilling to badmouth someone she barely knew.

Megan, never one to shy away from awkward situations, decided to take matters into her own hands. She waved Denise over, and the friendly waitress approached with a warm smile.

"Hey there, ladies! How're ya doin' Megan? What can I get ya?" Denise greeted them.

Megan introduced her friends, and Denise took their orders. She was easygoing and amiable, and Ashley was dying to ask her about knowing Corey, but said nothing.

"Wait around for the music set," Denise suggested, her eyes twinkling. "Our guy, Corey, is about to start."

Ashley's suspicions fought against Denise's word choice: *our* guy.

Just as the clock neared 7:30, the entrance to the bar swung open, and a rush of cool evening air swept in. Corey hurried inside, clutching his guitar case, his gaze scanning the crowd. Oblivious to Ashley's presence in the corner, he made his way to a small stage at the far end of the room.

With a confident flourish, Corey got out his guitar and adjusted the microphone. The anticipation in the room crackled as patrons called out requests and conversed with one another. He sang song after song, mostly country, but a few that were pop. Ashley knew he was good, but here, on stage, in front of what looked like fans, he was positively astounding.

Then, amid the applause, someone in the crowd shouted for a love song.

Corey paused for a moment. A subtle change crossed his face as he mulled over the suggestion.

"Well," he said, his voice deep through the microphone, "I'm workin' on one. It's not polished yet, but maybe y'all can give me some feedback." With a deep breath, he began to play, his fingers expertly coaxing soulful chords from the strings. His voice, rich and evocative, filled the room.

The opening notes of the song hung in the air, haunting and beautiful, drawing the attention of everyone in the Circle Bar including the staff. Ashley's girlfriends, who had been giggling and teasing moments before, fell silent, captivated by the mesmerizing melody.

Corey sang with all his heart, pouring raw emotion into the lyrics. His gaze scanned the room, connecting with faces in the crowd, unaware that the girl who had inspired the song sat hidden in the corner, blocked by a woman with flaming red hair.

The song unfolded like a heartfelt confession, each word an intimate revelation. It was a breathtaking serenade, an unspoken plea, the strains of a heart laid bare. And as the final note echoed in the dimly lit bar, Corey couldn't have known that he had sung his soul's deepest desire to the one who held his heart.

Ashley gulped.

Chapter 16

THE FINAL NOTE of Corey's song hung in the air, a melody that had quieted the usually boisterous patrons of the Circle Bar. He carefully placed his guitar back into its case, his emotions still high. That's when Emma and Megan approached him, a glint of mischief in their eyes.

"Your biggest fan is sitting over there," Megan said, her lips curling into an impish smile.

Confused, Corey followed their gaze, his heart doing somersaults in his chest when he spotted Ashley, sitting at the corner table. The shock, embarrassment, and surprise mingled on his face as he realized that she had been there, listening to him pour his heart out in song.

Determined not to let this moment slip away, he maneuvered through the crowd, reaching Ashley before she could leave. Several emotions and a whole lot of adrenaline made his heart race, but he managed a smile as he approached.

"Hey, Ashley," he greeted her, slightly breathless. He nodded politely at the friend with her.

The friend, Julia, complimented his singing, "You were amazing," and, excusing herself, left them alone. Corey turned his attention to Ashley, her eyes reflecting confusion and anticipation. He cleared his throat, gathering his thoughts.

"Hey," he said, his voice as steady as he could make it. "I didn't know you were here."

"And I had no idea you were the main entertainment here. None of the guys at the ranch said anything."

"Only Jet knew I'd be here tonight."

"Oh."

There seemed a shift in the atmosphere. Corey's eyes locked onto Ashley's, and he felt exposed, like a fragile piece of glass waiting to shatter. He took a deep breath, fighting the nervousness that threatened to overtake him.

"I wanted to explain a bit about the song," he began, his voice sincere and gentle. "I messed with some of the lyrics because, well, it was about you."

Ashley blinked, her eyes widening. "Me?"

Corey barely bobbed his head, his fingers fidgeting with the bandana tied around his wrist. "Yeah. I wanted to capture how I felt, but I was nervous ... so, after our picnic, I changed a few words. And then, well, you were sort of chilly toward me ... and I reworded the song again."

Her gaze shifted, occasionally flicking toward the waitress serving a nearby table. Something changed in her demeanor, and he could see something—relief?—wash over her.

"I thought ... I thought you were seeing someone else," she admitted, a hitch in her voice.

Corey's heart ached at her words. He took a step closer, gently taking her hand. "No, Ashley. You've been on my mind, in my heart. I haven't felt this way about anyone before. That picnic meant a lot to me, and I'd like to spend more time with you, get to know you better."

He hoped the sincerity in his voice touched her; he thought he felt her hand relax.

A smile played on Ashley's lips, and she squeezed his hand. "I'd like that too, Corey."

Chapter 17

A SHLEY FELT HER worries immediately dissolve. The strains of the song still lingered in her mind, his honest confession of feelings were things she felt, too. Corey's courage and honesty had warmed her heart, dispelling any doubts.

In that moment, under the soft glow of the Circle Bar lights, their hearts connected, their emotions blending like the verses of that sweet melody.

"Really," she said, "I'd like that a lot."

Corey beamed. "Let's get outta here, huh?"

As Ashley drove away from the Circle Bar with Corey following her in his truck, her heart felt light, full of the promise of their budding romance. She'd been wrong about Denise. Obviously, the text made sense now. The earnest words of Corey's serenade still filled her heart, and she couldn't wait to spend more time with him.

The winding road stretched ahead, the darkness pierced by the glow of her headlights. A single car passed her, weaving as if the driver were drunk or texting, the taillights soon dissolving. The stars above were barely visible through the thick canopy of clouds. Corey's vehicle trailed behind her as they headed to the ranch along the otherwise deserted road.

A pair of blinding headlights appeared, rapidly closing the distance between them. Panic surged through her veins as she realized the oncoming vehicle was not slowing down.

She swerved her car to the side, narrowly avoiding a devastating collision. Then, in her rearview mirror, Ashley saw the nightmare unfold. The truck veered directly into Corey's path. In an instant, her world shattered as the truck collided with Corey's vehicle, sending it spinning off the road. The sound of metal against metal reverberated through the night, along with the sickening screech of tires and the terrifying crunch of impact.

Panic surged through her veins, her chest constricting with fear. She stomped on the brakes, her car skidding to a stop. She fumbled for her phone and dialed 911, her voice frantic as she relayed their location.

"Please, there's been an accident. We need help," she pleaded into the phone.

With trembling hands, she jumped out of her car and rushed to the scene. Fear gripped her as she surveyed the wreckage, her eyes locking onto Corey's truck. It had been thrown off the road, resting at an unnatural angle, its mangled frame evidence of the violence of the collision.

She called out Corey's name and approached the wreckage, her heart pounding. When she reached the truck, her worst fears were realized. Corey had been thrown from the vehicle and lay sprawled on the ground, unconscious and unmoving.

Tears welled up in her eyes as she knelt beside him. *Should I touch him? No, I mustn't move him. Please don't be dead.* She gently touched him, trying to rouse him without moving him, but he remained unresponsive.

The driver of the other vehicle, a disheveled and inebriated man, staggered along the highway, heading in the opposite direction. His voice slurred as he repeated the last line of Corey's love song over and over, creating an eerie and haunting backdrop to the nightmarish scene.

Ashley started crying then. She couldn't help herself. She stared at Corey's lifeless form and clung to the hope that help would arrive soon. She prayed for a miracle.

Chapter 18

COREY'S EYELIDS FLUTTERED open, and for a moment, he was disoriented. The sterile scent of the hospital room and the dull hum of machinery told him where he was. The room felt both suffocating and comforting as he gradually awoke, his head heavy and his body aching. He tried to sit up, but a jolt of pain shot through his left wrist, making him wince. Confusion briefly clouded his thoughts, but it lifted as Ashley leaped up from the chair she'd been occupying all night.

"Corey, you're awake!" she exclaimed, her eyes shining with relief.

"Ashley?" he croaked, his voice hoarse.

He managed a weak smile, his gaze shifting to the cast that immobilized his left wrist and hand. Panic threatened to rise as he realized the extent of his injuries. "What happened?"

She quickly filled him in on the details of the accident, how she had called 911, and the subsequent events that brought him to this hospital room. Corey listened intently, grateful that she had been there for him throughout the night.

Ashley gently recounted the accident, her voice soothing as she assured him the doctor said his concussion was not serious.

"But my hand?"

"Um, yeah, it's bad. They're bringing in a hand specialist. You'll need surgery."

Anxiety gnawed at him as the possibility of not playing the guitar again was his first and only thought.

As he absorbed the information, the door swung open, and two familiar faces entered. Jet and Dawn, wearing concerned expressions, hurried over to Corey's bedside.

"We've been praying for you, buddy," Jet said with a warm smile.

"Yeah, we missed your silly face at breakfast," Dawn added, setting a plate of brownies on the bedside table. "I made these for you."

"Thanks."

They chatted a bit and then the doctor walked in, a no-nonsense look on his face. He checked Corey's vital signs and then turned his attention to his bandaged head and wrist. He spoke slowly, giving Corey a dose of reality as he discussed the extent of the injuries.

"Mr. Johnson, I have some news," the doctor said, his tone serious. "Your left wrist and fingers were severely injured in the accident. You'll need intensive therapy to regain full function. It won't be easy, but with time—six weeks or so—and effort, you should be able to hold the reins adequately."

"And play the guitar?"

"Hmm, that may take some fine-tuning, pardon the pun. And more than six weeks."

Corey felt a mix of relief and apprehension. He glanced at his left hand, his fingers encased in a temporary cast, and the reality of the situation sank in.

"As long as I can play again, I'll do whatever it takes," Corey replied, determination in his eyes.

The doctor gave him a thorough account of what was involved in the surgery, who would do it, and that surgery was set for this afternoon.

Corey's heart sank yet again as he heard about the pain he would have to endure, the reality settling in of the long road to getting back to playing an instrument.

"Don't worry," Dawn said. "We've got a whole church full of people ready to pray you back to health. Now, have a brownie. Or two. These will cheer you up."

Corey managed a weak grin. "Thanks, Dawn. I'm going to need some cheering up."

"Looks like you already have a cheerleader," Jet winked at Ashley. "We'll leave you two."

Chapter 19

WITH HIS ARM in a sling and a cast that covered his left arm from elbow to fingertips, Corey let out a huge exhalation as he was discharged from the hospital a couple of days later. Martha's kind offer to have him take her place and help Ashley teach the new riding students who were due to arrive the following Monday, provided him with a sense of purpose, something to look forward to, even if he couldn't fully participate in the ranch's regular work.

During the car ride back to the ranch, he thanked Martha, but fretted over how he'd pay the hefty hospital bills.

"I have a small inheritance, but it might not be enough."

"Don't worry. God will provide. He always does." Martha chuckled. "Remember how that mysterious benefactor helped me with the legal fees? He might come through for you, Corey. You never know."

A suspicion that Jet was her patron angel swirled in Corey's mind, but he didn't ask.

Upon his return to the ranch, he was greeted by Dawn and Ashley and fawned over like a new puppy. They accompanied him to the ranch's cozy living room, where he was ordered to rest while Dawn prepared supper.

As Corey sat in there, his injured arm in a sling and a confusion of feelings swirling in his head, Martha's offer that he work at the riding school got him thinking of one advantage. Teaching the new riding students seemed not only like the perfect way to contribute while recovering, but it would be time spent with or at least near Ashley.

He watched the vibrant hues of the sunset painting the sky outside, and his thoughts turned back to the hospital bill. He had more than a hunch that Jet was the ranch's angel. He couldn't shake the thought that the injured veteran was silently watching over them, providing aid in more ways than they knew. Despite his money worries, he couldn't deny the warmth of the ranch and the sense of family that surrounded him.

Dawn and Ashley joined him, their friendly banter distracting him. Dawn had prepared a hearty meal; the aroma of home-cooked food infused the air.

As the cowboys trickled in from the range for the evening meal, Corey's return became a cause for celebration. They greeted him with cheers and backslaps, making a jovial fuss about his return. Jokes and jibes flew around the table. Pete offered to help cut his meat, garnering chuckles from everyone.

"I've always got your back, buddy," Pete teased, a roguish glint in his eyes. "But for any other, uh, personal assistance you might need … well, we're gonna cut cards to see who helps you then."

The cowboys laughed and the women did too.

"No worries," Corey said, "I'm right-handed."

Corey smiled at the closeness of his ranch family, grateful for the bonds that had grown stronger during his time of need. No one mentioned his truck though and he'd been too preoccupied to ask if it had been towed to an auto repair place or to a junk yard. It was going to take a long time to earn enough to get it fixed or, heaven forbid, buy another.

Chapter 20

THE WEATHER WAS just the right blend of crisp air and warm sunshine a few days later as Corey and Ashley prepared for their first riding therapy class. They stood in the corral, surrounded by eager kids and gentle horses, ready to introduce them to the joy of riding.

"All right, kids," Corey said, a smile lighting up his face. "Meet your new four-legged friends. This is Tango, and that's Star. Here's Bella and this one's Keno. They're all saddled up courtesy of our friend Jet. See that man over there?" The kids looked toward the stable where Jet stood, wearing cut-off jeans that revealed his prosthetic. He waved at the kids and then disappeared into the barn.

Ashley showed the children how to approach the horses gently. She took them one by one, but none understood the concept of 'gentle;' their enthusiasm was infectious. Luckily the well-trained horses accepted it. The kids, whether in wheelchairs, on crutches, or otherwise in need of help, were eager to interact with the horses, touching their soft muzzles and giggling with delight.

With patience, Ashley explained the basics of horseback riding to the children and their parents, focusing on building trust and communication with the horses.

She demonstrated mounting a horse, but each child was helped up the handicap mounting ramp Chris and Pete had constructed and helped onto the horse's back. Corey walked to the horse's other side and motioned the parent over to act as a spotter. The kids' faces lit up as they felt the gentle swaying motion; their laughter filled the air. One by one, they were led around the corral, their small hands gripping the saddle's pommel.

"All right, kids, remember to be kind to your new friend. No kicking them." Corey said. Not a single kid had asked him about his arm.

As the therapy class progressed, the challenges became apparent. Some kids faced fear or anxiety, but Corey and Ashley were patient, offering words of encouragement and including the parents for assistance. Slowly, they built trust and confidence, making progress that warmed their hearts. But, as with any new endeavor, there were hiccups along the way. A few kids became anxious, and one horse, Keno, got spooked, flicking his ears to express his annoyance. Corey quickly intervened, reassuring both horse and rider.

Once the session ended and the kids had left with their parents, Corey and Ashley set to work unsaddling the horses.

"I'll do it," Ashley said. "You just be careful not to bump your hand on anything."

Corey attempted to help despite his injury, but soon found it impossible to unbuckle, uncinch, or unlatch anything one-handed let alone pull the saddle off and carry it. He hollered for Jet, who came out of one of the stalls and lent a hand. When finished Jet and Ashley put the horses in their stalls and then Ashley walked out of the barn with Corey.

"You know," Corey began with a grin, "I think those kids taught me more today than I taught them."

Ashley chuckled. "I have to agree. It's amazing how these horses bring out the best in people. That was actually a lot of fun."

"It was. Did you hear the red-headed kid call me Corny?"

"I did. I think it might become your new nickname."

Their laughter turned into a tender moment, and Corey gazed at Ashley with affection as he walked her toward the ranch porch. "You made this seem like a breeze. You're a natural teacher."

She grinned, satisfaction written all over her face. "Well, thank you. It's a breeze with you around."

They reached the porch. Corey longed for a chance to kiss Ashley properly, but his injured arm posed a challenge. He mustered up the courage before they went in, their lips meeting in a clumsy, affectionate collision. The gesture became a bit comical due to Corey's sling, but it only added to the sweet memory.

"Oops," Corey murmured, laughing as he struggled with the sling.

Ashley giggled, her eyes filled with warmth. "I think we need a redo."

Their moment was interrupted by Martha, who arrived with the mail.

Corey opened a bill from the hospital, expecting the worst. To his surprise, it was already paid off. He looked at Ashley in astonishment, completely confused. Just then, a rumbling noise coming up the drive caught their attention.

A brand-new truck was being delivered.

Martha shook her head and smiled. "Looks like our ranch angel's at it again."

Chapter 21

I N THE COZY office in the barn, with the scent of horses and leather and hay in the air, Jet and Martha huddled over blueprints spread across the desk. The soft glow of the desk lamp illuminated their faces, expressions serious and thoughtful as they discussed the future of Double Horseshoe Ranch.

"Jet, these plans are exceptional," Martha remarked, tracing her finger over the lines. "The indoor arena would be a game-changer for the riding school."

Jet nodded, quite enthused. "And the additional barn will allow us to expand the boarding services for more horses. Plus, the cottage for Dawn and me would be perfect."

"It would," Martha agreed, a smile forming. "It's a wonderful dream, but I haven't the money for any of this. Sure, the price of beef has gone up, but …"

"I'll pay for it all." Jet balanced more on his good leg and leaned a hand on the desk. "If you haven't guessed …"

"I thought so. It was you who paid the lawyers."

"Guilty."

"And were you the anonymous benefactor with that crazy marriage proposal?"

"Guilty again. I meant it as a practical joke and I guess I became the butt of that joke. A very happy butt, though." He laughed heartily. "But let's keep that between us."

"Sure."

"Anyway, I'd like to buy into the Double Horseshoe. Maybe be a half-owner. I have a huge trust fund that I gain complete control of January first." He chuckled. "Name your price."

Martha, without a moment's hesitation, did.

Jet grinned. "That sounds fair. Any conditions?"

"Yes, having you handle the financial side and growth strategies would really lift a weight off my shoulders."

"Done."

Martha smiled, extending her hand. They shook hands, sealing their commitment to a new beginning.

Later, during supper, the ranch hands gathered around the long table. Jet stood, raising his glass. "I've got some exciting news to share. Martha and I have decided to join forces. I'll be part owner of the ranch."

Applause and cheers erupted along with some stage whispers about Jet's rich father which Jet and Martha ignored.

Instead, Jet grinned. "And before you make any jokes about me abandoning Dawn for a slightly older woman, let me assure you that Dawn and I are still getting married New Year's Day. But we'd like to celebrate this milestone with a party next week—half engagement party and half partnership party."

"Cool," Sawyer said, "and we can party till the cows come home. Literally."

Jet cleared his throat. "There's more. I want to build an indoor riding arena for the school, another barn for the additional horses we'll be boarding, and a cottage for Dawn and me. I'll handle more of the financial side of things, and Martha can help Dawn with the school once Corey gets back to riding and rustling."

Martha's face lit up with a pleased smile. "I can't tell you all how happy I am about this. It's a fantastic idea. Tell them about the blueprints, Jet."

Chapter 22

THE SUN DIPPED below the horizon as Corey and Ashley leaned against the sturdy corral fence. Supper had ended, the excitement about the building plans had calmed down, and a sense of contentment filled the air along with the melodies of chirping crickets.

Corey gazed into Ashley's eyes, his heart pounding. "Ashley, there's something I've been wanting to ask you."

Her eyes sparkled with anticipation as she turned to face him. "What is it, Corey?"

He took a deep breath, his voice sincere and earnest. "Would you consider being my girl? I promise I'll only ever write songs for you."

A radiant smile bloomed on her face, and without hesitation, she threw her arms around him in a tight embrace. Corey winced slightly, but Ashley immediately pulled back, her eyes filled with concern.

"I'm so sorry," she exclaimed. "I forgot about your cast."

Corey chuckled, his heart warming at her sweet apology. "No need to apologize. Once this cast is off, you can expect to squeeze me tighter than a saddle cinch."

Her laughter rang out like a melody, and she leaned closer. "I'll hold you to that."

"You better." He stared at her a moment. "So, uh, was that your answer?"

"Corey," Ashley's eyes reflected the setting sun, "I've been thinking about our relationship, and I am ready to take the leap. I'll be your girl. Will you be my guy?"

A warmth flooded Corey's heart as he looked into her eyes. "Ashley, you bet I will."

An owl hooted its approval in the distance.

Corey, his voice cracking with excitement, asked, "Would you like to hear the song I've been working on since the hospital?"

Ashley nodded. He swallowed violently, his Adam's apple seizing and jumping. He cleared his throat and began to sing:

"In the starlight's gentle gleam,
You're the girl of my every dream.
With every note, with every rhyme,
You've captured this heart of mine.

Through days of blue or gray,
With you, I'll find my way.
In the dark and stormy night,
You're my beacon, my guiding light.

Hand in hand, we'll find our way,
In love's embrace, come what may.
In your eyes, I've found my home,
With you, I'll never be alone."

As he sang, Corey's gaze never left Ashley's face. When he finished, he pulled her into a gentle, one-armed embrace. This kiss was sweet and pure and held a promise they hadn't spoken.

THE END

Want more?

Their stories aren't over yet. In book 3 of the *Hearts Unbridled* series, A COWBOY'S PROMISE, we get through the Montana winter with several big events (maybe a wedding or two? maybe a break-up? maybe a catastrophe?) and one new romance. Ashley's friend, Julia, has had her eye on one of the cowboys, strong and silent Chris, since before the rodeo. When a disaster means she has to stay at the ranch for a spell, there's a chance for her to get to know him better, but new ranch hire, Blake, gets in the way. Find A COWBOY'S PROMISE only on Amazon.